HIDDEN IN LORE

An Elven Heritage Collection

CHRISSY WISSLER

Blue Cedar Publishing

ALSO BY CHRISSY WISSLER

Elven Heritage Series

Hidden in Mist

Hidden in Truth

Hidden in Shadow

Hidden in Fire

Hidden in Flight

Hidden in Spirit

Hidden in Desire

Hidden in Memory

Hidden in Time: Novel

Hidden in Lore: Collection #1

Hidden in Myth: Collection #2

Hidden in Legend: Collection #3

Little League Series

Swing Away: A Little League Novel

Prom Dates & Softball Bats

Throw Like a Girl, Catch a Date

Fly Away

No Crying in Softball

More to Life than Softball

A Pitcher's Unexpected Date

A Catcher's Christmas Wish

Stolen Bases, Stolen Kisses

Softball Baby

INTRODUCTION

Like many dreamers and young readers, I grew up on Tolkien. I remember, in the fourth grade, sneaking in my library's hard-backed copy of the *The Hobbit*. You know, that edition with the green and dark-blue jacket, almost a purple-like color, showing with these limited colors just a snippet of Tolkien's world and that windy road up to the Lonely Mountain. How I sat there at my desk, arms covering the book and trying to read without being seen by my teacher or classmates. (I'm fairly certain the other kids saw—and just didn't care. It was, after all, *just* a book.)

But there were often, a number of times, where I just held the book. As if that act alone, simply having it beside me, meant I was still in that world of dragons and dwarves and archers named Bard...

And no longer in this one.

Tolkien took me and held me there in his magical world of hobbits and dwarves and elves, and my dreaming mind (because what kid *actually* pays attention in school) until I started creating my own worlds. My own magic. My own romance. My own heroic adventures which were so very, very far from the girl I actually was.

Yet, my love of all things elves and history, really, stayed with me.

To the point where all the way into college and after, a question tugged at me:

What if elves really *had* existed?

And what if they had simply... disappeared?

This idea took the initial form of a some place down in New Zealand, which made complete sense because at the time, Tolkien's stories were coming alive right before our eyes with Peter's Jackson's *The Lord of the Rings* movies. Those movies came and went and changed my life in profound ways (I can barely believe it's nearly been twenty years), and I kept on dreaming. My own life changed had its share of bumps along the way until I found my way back to stories and my writing...

And again, that question...

What if elves had existed?

And truly, I believed they did. At some point. Somewhere place. Some place. I felt it, right there in my soul.

So, when I left my full-time job to write as much as humanly possible before we started our family (to which I knew, darn well, children would set my writing production to just about nothing—which, it did, and deservedly so).

But that same question wouldn't leave me...

Instead, it stayed and slowly changed form. Slowly became the voice of a young girl, who stood in that really weird, really annoying (and uncomfortable) time between childhood and... almost, adulthood. Stubborn and almost desperate to find herself, especially when everything about her was just *different*.

While I, myself, am not an elven descendant, I'd like to think that my spirit is, and it was this spirit who eventually found her way into this story, and brought me Kate.

Kate, a name I loved so much, that we named our daughter this.

And while the two girls have nothing in common, they certainly share the same stubbornness and desire to find their own way (and damn anyway else telling them otherwise). Which, means I've got myself an interesting road as a parent (at the writing of this, my daughter, is only five), as well as an interesting road as a writer...

I haven't a clue where Kate and her story will take me, or the lost elves and their magic. I simply started writing and let Kate show me the way. This series started as short stories, little bits all strung together until even those started to take shape and become something else entirely. It only seemed fitting that they belong here, in this collection, together. There are many more stories to come, more twists and turns and unexpected moments. But this here is the start of Kate and her journey, into learning who she is and answering that so important question:

Who am I?

I hope you come on this journey with me, as together we journey into the past to find out exactly what happened to those lost elves Tolkien had believed in so much...

The same ones that just might have lived outside our own front doors.

—Chrissy Wissler
Torrance, CA
March, 2018

HIDDEN IN MIST

An Elven Heritage Short Story

HIDDEN IN MIST

There was no way Kate was setting foot in that forest.

Not with those pines...those trees practically drenched in mist. No, as if the mist were seeping from their trunks and branches.

As if they were one and the same.

Their needles so dark they looked almost black. Disappearing right into that mist and farther up...so far up she couldn't see where the trees stopped and the sky began.

That gray, moody sky.

If she just gave it a minute, she was sure it'd open up and drop buckets of water on her, her mom, and this crazy idea about hiking at Mount Rainier when, as far as she was concerned, it was still in the middle of winter.

Even if there was no snow...right at this particular spot.

Kate gripped the worn, fraying strap of her backpack. Hands cold, numbed. She almost wished for the heavy, pressing weight of books. Of her classmates. Of what they said behind her back.

Whispering.

Cold, unwelcoming eyes slanting towards her.

Just like that forest.

Not to mention the single, itsy-bitsy trail cutting into that forest—boot-packed dirt mostly covered with green stuff and leaves—that she was supposed to follow. As if this were no problem. Head right into the creepy forest that was sending her stomach twisting.

Making the hairs on her neck stand up on edge.

She felt it.

Really.

She wasn't crazy.

Those trees were actually bending towards her. She could hear the creaking of bark as it twisted.

Turned to her.

Her breath puffed out in a white, cloudy mist.

Her mom was crazy. Insane. This place was supposed to make her feel better?

But seriously, if the creepy factor wasn't gonna clue her mom in, you'd think the emergency vehicles and rescue guys behind her would do the trick.

But no.

Not her mother.

Kate glanced over her shoulder. The dozens of men and even a few dogs, making their way to the visitor center and back country office. Two buildings that looked like they'd fought tooth, nail, and floorboard for this spot in the forest. Their brown coat of paint, now flaking and peeling, was clearly the loser of that battle.

There were a lot of rescue workers, she noticed. All with strained faces. Conversations nonexistent.

Part of her wanted to know what had happened. Was it a rescue or a recovery?

But the other half, the part of her that looked at this forest, part of Mount Rainier and the National Park, with its misty claws and twisty trees, that half...didn't want to know.

Was afraid to know.

Every parking space was taken. Vans marked "Search and Rescue" parked on the squishy mountain grass. In between long, skinny trunks of pines. Squeezed in so close there was barely any room to open a door.

Felt just like this forest.

With all the trees.

Pressed around her. Bending towards her.

Reaching.

She wasn't imagining things...was she?

Kate's hands reached up. Automatically. Without thinking. Slipped free strands of blond hair from her ponytail. Covered her ears.

Different. Weird. Freak.

Kate shoved the memories—Heather's words—as far from her as she could. Stomped her boots. Her toes still numb even with the double layering of scratchy wool socks.

She was fine. Totally normal.

There was nothing wrong with her.

Just like there was nothing wrong with the creepy forest of doom.

She gave that forest another look before turning, half hoping she could convince her mom this wasn't such a great idea.

Not that the three-hour drive from Seattle had done a thing. Seattle, where they'd been living only a few short months before the whispers started again and her mom, as usual, got this strange look on her face. This constant uneasiness that drained her of color, making her look all hollow-like. At least until she'd decided to come on this stupid hike in the first place and then bam, there was rosiness in her cheeks again.

Which still didn't change the fact that in a month, maybe two, her mom would throw in the towel and they'd head back to Montana. 'Cause no matter what her mom did, she couldn't escape.

Kate headed up the gravel road—which turned into a cobblestone path (though, to be honest, at least half the stones were MIA). There was her mother, fully decked out in hiking gear (which Kate hadn't known they'd even owned), sporting a warm, purple jacket with matching pants. A jacket that hugged her curves in all the right places...nothing like Kate's bulging jacket, which had a thing for making her look like a whale and not like a filling out (slowly) teenage girl.

Her mother, who was determined—for whatever reason—to see this little mother-daughter hike through.

Even though her mother hated the forest. Hated trees.

Except right now. Apparently.

Her mom was making her way closer to the command center (the only park visitor that Kate could see) and the thick throng of rescue guys in jackets (bulkier than hers, if it were possible). They didn't seem to notice her mom. Not with walkie-talkies glued to their hands and all eyes focused on the linebacker standing in front of a map, leading the charge.

A map that had a couple dozen pins of different colors. None, Kate had a feeling, that were good.

Her chest tightened. Felt like her heart squeezed between beats.

Why couldn't they just leave? Forget this stupid trip that was doing —absolutely—nothing to help Kate forget. Couldn't. Not when she could easily hear the visitor center's creaking welcome sign. Could hear it so well, it was as if she stood underneath it and not at the tail end of the parking lot. Or the muted, hushed conversation taking place at the command center as plans were made for another day of search. And recovery.

To find the missing girl.

Alice.

That was her name. A girl who'd been last seen near Indian Henry's Hunting Ground Trail, following right behind her friends, and then was gone. No trace. No sign. Nothing.

Kate bit her lip. Tried to keep from listening.

Couldn't.

Just like before. With Heather, who she'd thought, even for a moment, was her friend. Not best friend, but the first person who'd given Kate a smile and showed her where her locker was, and home-room, and the fastest way out of school as soon as the ear-splitting bell rang.

The tall man with pretty impressive football shoulders, sporting a piratical eye patch, stepped forward, and the rest of the Search and Recovery group came to him. Silent, watchful, as if they were all under some sort of spell. Probably fear for the girl. Alice. His face was a road map of wrinkles and scars, one jagged one running right through his eyebrows and straight on down. She'd a feeling there was no eye there, just an eye patch. Why she thought that, or why she just *knew*, she had no idea. It was just a feeling, just this... certainty.

"We've searched the twenty-three miles where Alice was last seen," he said. "Both man- and dog-teams. The kids say she was last spotted here."

He pointed to a blue pin, finger just as huge as those arms.

"So far, the canines haven't caught a scent. No sign either. Not anywhere off the trail. No broken branches. No footprints."

He focused his attention on each man and then the one or two women awaiting their orders. Then stopped suddenly. Kate realized her mother lingered on the outskirts of the group, just outside of normal hearing range, but he wasn't looking at her mother.

No. He was looking at Kate.

Saw Kate, and only Kate.

Single eye met hers. Green or gray or hazel...she couldn't tell, the color kept shifting.

But his gaze didn't. It held right there, right on her, and he just kept on staring across the heads of all his workers as if he knew...

That she could hear.

Kate swerved on her boots, digging into that half cobblestone, half gravel path. Fast. She dug her now-numb hands deeper into her jacket pockets as if all that would stop the voices. As if she ran far enough and stuck her fingers in her ears, it would all go away.

Poof.

Like magic.

His voice continued, following her. "The helicopter hasn't seen her either. It'd help if the weather held, but that fog..."

Deep. Baritone. As if it knew it was delivering bad news but did it anyway. Had to.

"I'll be honest. It's not looking good."

Kate's throat closed. Locked the air in her chest. Even as the fear tightened. Held on.

It was happening again. Just like at school.

Kate made a beeline for the bathroom. Passed the half-collapsed wood bench with its neon-green moss covering it from top to bottom. Practically ran across the cobblestone path with its missing stones.

She didn't care. She kept running.

All that mattered were flushing toilets, locking stalls, and being at the other end of the visitor center. Away, far away, from the rescue center.

But then she heard another sound. Slow, shuffling boots over squishy grass, but lighter, not as heavy as the rescue workers, because these were made by younger someones. Half their age. Her age, in fact. She could tell all this just by the sound of boots sticking to the moist earth, almost as if the earth, the forest, wanted them to stay.

Wanted to keep them.

Kate looked back, stopped. Couldn't help herself. And, she'd been right: they were her age. All of them maybe a year or two older, but definitely seniors, while she was just squeaking in as a junior. They didn't look like anyone at her school, though, not the way their bodies shuffled along, as if they were sleepwalking as they came out of a small wooden building. It was as if their bodies were moving but they hadn't quite realized it. Eyes red-rimmed. Black circles fading into eye sockets. Haggard. Exhausted.

Seeming to fade right before her eyes, as if all the colors that belonged to them were disappearing.

Kate picked up her pace. Needed to. But she wasn't fast enough, couldn't get far enough.

Because she heard them just fine too.

How they should have watched out for Alice. Kept her partnered up with someone. Given her a compass instead of making her lug the extra water as a joke. Should have stayed put, together, when the fog rolled in instead of hiking through it, even when it covered the ground, the trees, until all they could see was the murky grayness.

And shadows.

Kate squeezed her eyes closed. She wasn't hearing any of this. Couldn't be.

Except she was.

"There you are," her mother said.

With Kate's head bent low—not to mention her closed eyes (probably not the smartest of moves)—she nearly walked right into her mother. Who had appeared before Kate. Silent.

As if she'd materialized right out of thin air.

Kate slid to a stop.

Sort of.

Her boot, barely broken in as it was, caught on some stone—one of the handful of stones actually still in the path. She pitched forward, would have gone headfirst into the rain-soaked, mushy grass if her mother hadn't caught her.

Easily.

Gracefully.

So nothing at all like Kate.

"Oh! There, there. You're all right. So clumsy, my Kate, even now."

Her mom stood there, a hesitant, almost relieved smile on her face even as she righted Kate. How was it possible that they were related—mother, daughter—and yet her mom looked as if she was meant to be there, like as if was comfortable in her body, with who she was?

Nothing at all like Kate.

"I'm sorry. I thought you heard me."

"I didn't," Kate muttered. "Hear you, I mean."

"Oh, well. That's good." Again, there was the smile.

Which was weird. Because her mom was the one person whom Kate never seemed to hear. Not that she told her mom that. Or about the kids at school...every school she ever went to. No, it was better to keep it to herself, better to just try and hide and blend in. Her mom wouldn't understand, not as graceful and beautiful as she was. And besides, not hearing her mom was a good thing, right? Like, maybe she wasn't a freak; maybe all her classmates were wrong about her.

It should have made her feel better.

It didn't.

Not when Kate was finally starting to piece together these little oddities. Starting to wonder...about herself. About her mom.

What if Heather was right?

"I'm...glad we're here," her mom said.

She sure as heck didn't look glad.

"It's been a while since I've been hiking. Maybe I missed it."

Again, didn't look like she missed it.

"Anyway, this will be good for you too. To get away from your friends, from school. Clear your mind."

Kate knew, simply knew, that her mom was lying to her. This whole impromptu trip was a lie. She didn't know how or why, just that it was. Her mom hated the forest. Anything that looked like a tree, even if it was only two feet high, she wanted nothing to do with. And yet, the moment she'd heard about Heather at school (not from Kate) telling everyone how weird Kate was, how she'd overheard a private conversation, one that had been impossible to hear, her mom had swooped on in and plucked Kate right out of there.

And then insisted they come here, to Mount Rainer.

Her mom patted Kate's arms, wiping away invisible dirt or dust or whatever that brown stuff decked out all over the ground was, acting as if Kate were covered in it, when she wasn't.

"And you should be more careful," her mom said. "I don't want you to get hurt. A lot can happen out here, you know."

It was almost as if her mom couldn't stop moving, as if she was nervous.

"I want to go home," Kate said. "I don't like this place."

Her mom's hands finally slowed. Stilled.

"I know, sweetie, I know. It's...a little uncomfortable at first. But I think you need to be here."

"Why?"

"I just...I just know. And who knows, maybe we'll both get some answers and figure out what we want to do next."

Right. As if that wasn't a dodge.

"Sure, Mom, whatever." Kate pushed her away. "As if being in this creepy forest is going to give me all the answers, like how to stop the whole school saying I'm weird. That I'm a freak when we both know I am."

It was the first time, ever, she'd said this to her mom. But she couldn't help it. Her chest hurt as if it was just going to tear right open.

"That wasn't what I—"

But Kate wasn't listening. She was heading back to the car...with or without her mom.

She couldn't stay here. Had to run. Had to get far, far from this freaky forest with its tall, reaching and bending trees. From her mother who knew—knew—why she was weird, why she wasn't normal like everyone else, and still pretended otherwise. Like how Kate could still hear those voices, the teens, whose words slapped and yapped at her steps, just like the soaking, water-moist ground. Mud and upturned grass that clung to her boots, refusing to let go.

Just like the voices.

"They won't tell us, but it's true."

It was a girl's voice, breaking, catching.

"They don't think they'll find Alice. Not alive."

Not alive.

Kate focused on breathing.

Her mom followed right behind her. Her mom, who didn't carry along the slurping, sucking of boots on grass like Kate did.

Or like any normal person did.

God, it was as if she couldn't be fully weird and cool and beautiful like her mom. No. Instead, she just had to be weird and gangly and just...just wrong.

"I know you don't like this, being here," her mom said. "I don't either. Trust me. We will go on this hike and be done with it. It will be good for you. You know I don't like trees much—"

"You hate them."

"Well, yes, but even still, I need to come out here to.. think. I did it when I was your age and it helped me understand."

"Are you going to tell me about it?"

Her mom stumbled a moment, which was a first.

"No."

"Fine. Then I'm going home."

"What I'm trying to say, please, just wait a moment."

She reached for Kate's arm but Kate jerked it away, smooth and graceful, which was so not Kate's normal mode.

Her mom huffed. "Okay, fine, I understand. You're mad. All I'm trying to say is the forest helped me move on, and besides, you're always asking to get away from the city, and—"

Oh my God! She just didn't to get it.

"What about that girl?" Kate asked.

"Girl? You mean Heather? Honey, I'm sure it was just a misunderstanding. She probably didn't realize just how close you were and I'm sure it was embarrassing, what you heard, to say the least. She'll forgive you once she realizes you only had her best interests—"

"I'm not talking about Heather!"

Kate stopped, kicking up clumps of dirt, and faced her mom. She snapped her hands on whale-shaped hips (thanks to the butt-ugly jacket). She just...just wanted to scream at her mother to actually listen to what she was saying.

To just tell her the truth already.

There was something weird about her. About this forest.

"Alice," Kate snapped. "I'm talking about the girl lost in the woods. Her name is Alice. You know, the girl who disappeared right before her friends in some strange fog? With shadows. Who those rescuer-guys aren't sure they can find. What if something like that happens again, huh? To me?"

"Alice?"

Her mom's had gone pale. Her face. Neck. Even her hands were bone-white.

"Where—where did hear that?"

"From over there...." Kate jerked her head to the command center.

Her mom followed the movement, eyes widening further.

She must be tracking the distance, calculating, trying to understand what Kate was saying....

Then she saw a brief moment of horror—no, fear—cloud her mom face.

"Are you telling me, that...that you could hear them?"

Oh, God. Hadn't she learned to keep her mouth shut? Hadn't school and Heather and everyone before taught her anything?

"I mean," Kate muttered, "I just overheard it, when I was passing by."

"Katherine Silver. Can you hear them?"

Kate's shoulders shot back. Back taut and straight. "And what if I could? What would you do then? Tell me the truth? Explain why everyone, even my closest friend, thinks I'm a freak?"

"You're not a freak. There's nothing wrong with you."

Except her mom closed her eyes. Shivered.

There was a sudden gust of wind. Cold. Biting. As if it had been carried right on down the slopes of Mount Rainier to slice through this small glade, this small opening in a forest that wasn't happy...as if that unhappiness had actually come even further, as if across a great, great distance.

And yet...it was this forest, this one right here, that didn't want them here, didn't want Kate here. She didn't know how she knew, she just knew, right down to her bones. Because...she was different.

"Mom," she whispered. "You know, don't you? You know what's wrong with me."

But her mom didn't answer. Not really.

Not like Kate expected anything else.

"There's...there's nothing wrong with you. And besides, what else would I do, huh? If you were so very different from everyone else? I would go on. We'd go on. Together. Just like we're going to do with this hike."

"That wasn't what I asked."

"I know."

Her mom reached out. Tugged one of Kate's free strands of hair, but didn't tuck it behind her ear. Instead, she just left it there...to hang. To cover that slight, delicate tip of her ear, barely different than anyone else's, but enough.

She didn't meet Kate's gaze.

"This is the only way," her mom said. "Trust me."

The only way.

Her words hummed in Kate's chest. Followed her. Licked at her boots the moment her feet finally touched that winding, half-eaten path—which her mom had the nerve to call a "trail." She glanced back at the visitor center one last time, at all the those rescue workers, the teens who looked drawn and faded, until her gaze landed on the one-eyed man who was, even now, watching her.

The need to run came over her again. It hit so hard and fast her knees practically buckled. Would have, if her mom hadn't been standing there. Beside her. Digging her fingers into that whale-shaped down jacket.

Keeping her upright.

As if she'd known.

She gazed down at Kate with that same strained smile she'd plastered on since they drove into the park. Since Kate had "told" her about the voices.

"See?" her mom said. Whispered. As if she didn't want to draw any attention. "There's nothing to be afraid of. We'll go on our hike and those boys will find that girl."

Kate doubted it. Just like she doubted her mom—very much—that there was nothing to fear.

A forest with pine trees so thick Kate couldn't see where one ended and another began. Their long, spindly limbs bowing down, deep green moss hanging off branches in long tendrils, practically touching the trail.

"It'll be fine." Her mom patted Kate's shoulder. "You'll see. We'll go on our hike, get some fresh air, and get some answers."

And yet, she still didn't say *what* answers, and Kate knew, without a doubt, that she never would.

At least if her mom could help it.

Her mom trudged into that forest without a backward glance. Her back so straight and tall it was as if someone—probably a tree—were pulling her by the hair to keep her upright, to keep her going. As if the very last thing she wanted in the world was to go in there, yet she went anyway.

Kate had no choice but to follow...and hoped to God they'd be out soon.

Before the forest decided to eat them. Just like it had Alice.

As far as Kate was concerned, this forest really had it out for her.

She tossed her backpack—smudged from top to bottom in neon-green moss, mud, and something that she was absolutely not going to look at—over the second—*second*—giant-sized log that just happened to have fallen right onto the path.

Err, trail.

It was as if the forest really, really wanted her gone. Wanted her zipping out of that park without a second glance.

Except, of course, Kate had no freakin' choice.

She scrambled over the ucky, rotting log. Wished her legs were an inch or two longer, and did her very best to not look at the squirmy, scuttling things as they dove for safe hidey-places under rough bark and broken, moss-drenched limbs. Her pants, of course, caught on one of those branches and took a good chunk of bark with it—along with dirt and white, finger-sized sluggy-looking things, trailing a path of slime—

"Eww. Gross!" Kate slapped at her knees.

Not with her bare hands...that would be pointless.

She used her sleeve instead.

Pushed and wiped—anything to get the things off her. She also did her very best not to scream like a little girl. This was the worst, absolutely worst idea her mother had ever, ever had.

"What's wrong?"

Yes, her mom, who was a good league or so ahead of Kate, barely breaking a sweat and looking as if she'd just gone for a short jaunt in the woods because not a hair from her long, perfectly plaited braid was loose or out of place. She also didn't have any bugs crawling over her pants either. Her legs being the inch or two Kate had needed to clear the log.

"Nothing." Kate slapped at her knees. "I'm fine."

Totally fine. So fine she was ready to go home...even if that meant going back to school. Anything was better than this forest. With its bugs.

With eyes that tracked her every move. Every breath.

Kate shivered, and for once, it had nothing to do with the biting wind that cut down this trail like it owned it. Made those pine needles dance and twist and rustle.

She had no idea how her mom could stand it. Any of it. Acting like everything was A-Okay.

Up ahead, her mom adjusted her own backpack. Took a long drink from her canteen, and then gave Kate a smile. A warm one filled with a ton of relief.

"You're doing great, you know? We're almost done with the loop and then, then we can go home. We don't have to come back."

"Uh-huh. Sure."

Kate plucked leaves, pine needles, and spare chunks of bark from her ponytail. Yeah. Real great. She was a regular Mountain Woman. It wasn't until she pulled out a crumpled maple leaf that she paused. Realized that she'd not only heard her mom just fine...but her mom had heard her.

Kate's head snapped up. Mouth open. Could she hear her mom? From here? And did she...did she actually just tell her mom that she could?

"Mom?"

Her mom stood there, halfway down the trail and nearly out of sight. Face so pale her smile and all that warmth totally gone.

She just looked at Kate...not in horror, but in resignation. As if she'd tried so hard...to pretend, deny Kate didn't know, but in the end, she'd failed anyway.

Kate could hear her and now, well, now they both knew.

"Oh, Kate, I'm so sorry. For all of this."

"Sorry? Why do you have to be sorry? You know, instead of feeling sorry, why don't you just tell me what the hell is going on? You know, like who the hell I am, instead of lying—"

An eagle screamed.

Loud. Shrill. Desperate.

At least Kate thought it was an eagle. She didn't exactly have much experience in this whole nature department. But it sounded—no, felt —as if it was just overhead.

The forest, right then, it...changed. Shifted, became something else, something other. That same other she'd sensed back at the visitor center, listening to the one-eyed guy and his hunt for Alice. The forest, with its pines and deadened summer trees, crept closer. Branches bending. Creaking. A mist, no, a fog slunk around the downed log. Up and over. Kissed her ankles, raising to her knees.

Kate's grip on her backpack tightened.

She couldn't tear her eyes from the fog. So cold. Colder than the snow-heavy wind from the giant mountain itself.

A cold, which felt like death.

The fog touched her chin. Gentle. Inviting. Pulled her gaze upward to the sky.

To see.

Kate stared up into a sea of branches. Sharp, deep green pine needles. They danced and swayed as another cold wind ripped between them. Arched overhead as if they were one wave.

Or more like a hand...reaching for her.

She heard her mom in the distance.

Calling her name.

Yelling.

But it was only a dim hum, and fading by the minute.

The eagle screamed again. Sharper this time.

Kate saw a small opening between the needles, the fingers. Glimpsed brilliant white feathers.

Then, gone again.

But it was enough. Enough to break the cold, cold grip the forest had over her. The cold that had creaked into her arms, legs, into her mind. Into her heart.

She couldn't see her mom. Not the trail. Not even that granite boulder.

"Mom!"

Kate jumped forward. Tripped—over a gnarling, twisted root. One that hadn't been there before.

She fell. Couldn't stop herself. Not even when her hands, braced to catch her on the boot-trampled trail but instead...landed on a blanket of freezing cold fog.

And a soft, bleached field of moss.

Kate's whole weight—and apparently her backpack's—smacked into the ground and onto Kate's poor hands. Hands and wrists that were absolutely not meant to take that kind of pounding. Certainly not the tiny rocks and branch slivers that dug into her palms.

She immediately twisted, rolled onto her side to take the pressure off. Held her hands close to her chest and gazed upward into a world of smoky-gray fog.

No trees towered above her with moss dripping from its branches. No sun, either. Not even wind, or the breath of one.

She swallowed a yell.

Then, a cry.

Not so much because of her wrists (which hurt like something else), but because of where she wasn't.

She lay on a bed of moss. And it wasn't like the kind of moss she'd seen earlier all along their hike. The kind that glared so bright and green it could blind you, or looked like it'd glow when the lights went out. That moss, with its glow-worm feel, didn't look like this.

Not like this at all.

Kate leaned closer to the tiny leafed thing that hadn't a speck of color. As if its color was gone. Stolen.

Its life leached right out, leaving this gray, wilted thing behind.

It hadn't been a dream.

She wasn't on the trail. Not anymore.

She strained to see. To catch even the smallest hint of tree, the trail, or her mother. Nothing but fog. It clung to her hands, slithered into her mouth. Made her breath puff out in white, freezing mists.

"Mom?"

Her voice, quiet, shaky, echoed about the small moss field.

No answer.

Not even the stirring of moist earth drifted to her. Only this gray world stared back at her. Glared at her.

As if daring her to keep up hope.

Her hands brushed the hard, rough dirt and the color-bleached moss. She hugged her knees to her chest. Rocked.

She was alone. All alone.

Just like at school.

Could practically hear Heather, her voice whispering right into Kate's ear. Telling her again, and again, that no one would speak with her or dare be seen with her.

A freak.

Kate buried her head in her arms. Squeezed her eyes closed. Anything to keep out the rolling fog. The faded, gray world.

Anything to keep from remembering, anything to keep the

memory far away from her. But it leached right on out, just like her own color, and there was nothing she could do to stop it. Only relive it.

"How dare you?"

Heather had stormed into the girls' locker room. Brown eyes narrowed, red-rimmed, face blotched as if she'd been crying. As if... she'd been humiliated.

"How dare you say those things about me? About Kent?"

"I wasn't. I didn't—I'm sorry, but I just heard him. At the soccer field with the team and I-I didn't want to not tell you. That he was only using you for, for—"

For sex.

Heather's face got even redder.

"I tried telling you."

But she couldn't. Not when she saw how much Heather cared for Kent, and why would she listen to Kate? The new girl. The one who'd been around only for a few months. So, Kate'd told another of Heather's friends, someone she thought she could trust.

"That's it, then? You just 'heard' him say those things about me? From the stands? Seriously, Kate? You really think I'm going to believe that lie?"

Heather came forward. Slapped Kate so hard in the chest she felt it right to her bones. She stumbled back. The back of her head smacked into a metal locker. It hurt, but not as much as Heather's words.

Those cut deep.

"Or is what he said true? That you're just a liar. Or, are you some freak with superpower hearing?"

Kate didn't answer.

But the fog did.

It pulsed around her, creeping closer. Growing colder. Hummed to her, told her how Heather was no different than her mom. Her mom, who knew there was something...off about Kate.

Knew, and yet, didn't tell her.

Kate buried her head deeper. Felt herself falling further into the fog and not caring.

Why should she?

Why, when the people she cared about most abandoned her?

Wings ruffled. Fluttered.

Kate's eyes drifted opened. Slowly. As if she were shoving, pushing against a current determined to take her far, far from home. Her memory, the day with Heather, held on. Fought to stay with her.

She felt tears run hot down her cheeks.

Actually, it was the only thing she felt now. Her hands, numb. Feet too. Even her heart.

Kate lifted her hands. Even they looked dim. Fading. As if the fog was already workings its way into her. Deeper and deeper.

Was this what had happened to Alice? Was she even Alice anymore, or just some husk of herself, rocking herself back and forth in the gray moss and crying?

Crying.

Just like Kate.

Kate wiped her eyes. Then harder when the tears wouldn't stop.

Another fluttering of wings. Just above her? As if...they were growing more concerned. Desperate.

Kate pushed to her feet. Shoved her backpack behind her. Winced as the small cuts on her palms pulled and burned, and cursed. Well, if she could feel pain, if she could get mad, then she'd get through this.

Somehow.

Every step took concentration. Strength. As if she waded through a swamp of black, sucking, rotting tar—not the springy gray moss. Sweat dotted her forehead, beaded, and then got swept up by the touches of cold fog.

She shivered, but kept going. Focused on putting one foot in front of the other. Followed, as best she could, the sound of wings. Thought, maybe, she heard a soft sob in the distance.

Kate peered, but still just saw waves of gray rolling over moss and long-leafed bushes. No way to even tell if she was going in circles. Or heading towards the trail.

Another sob.

Softer this time.

Weaker.

Could it be...?

Kate turned in the direction of the sound. The fog swirled about her ankles. Became thicker. Harder to see—and that was saying something.

She tightened her grip on her backpack. The strap dug into her palm, imprinting it, helping her focus.

But Heather's words pulled at her again. Yanked her back. Wanted her to sink further into the fog and the mist, to forget everything but how she would never fit in, would never be normal.

"I never want to see you again. You're not welcome in this school, in my home. You should just go. Go!"

"What's worse?" Kate asked aloud, asked outside of her memory. Asked the words she'd been too afraid to say at the time. "That you believed I was lying? Or that I was telling the truth?"

Maybe Heather was right.

That she was different.

A freak.

But that didn't mean she had to give up. Not now.

Another sob drifted to her. Found a crack through that thick, gray fog. Drifted to her, then a rustle. Like leaves bending and parting.

Not Heather, Kate knew, because Heather wasn't here.

"Alice?"

A pause, then...

"Stop. Just stop. Please."

Kate's knees nearly buckled. Relief, so sweet and powerful, nearly undid her. Made her fear want to let loose because she actually wasn't alone in this nightmare gray world.

"Hold on!" Kate called back—or tried to. Her voice seemed lost, muffled by the mist. "I'm coming. Just, just keep making noise."

Any kind of noise.

But Alice heard. And she did.

"Just go away. I don't need to hear anymore. I can't hear anymore."

Alice's voice was definitely faint, but it was enough.

Enough for someone like Kate.

She trampled over moss. Nearly ran into a tree that practically materialized before her, swept up right out of that fog—but Kate was on her toes now. Desperation pulling at her, driving her.

She wasn't alone.

A small glade appeared. Surrounded by a ring of blacker-than-night trees with branches that were bowed so low they were scraping the back of a short, chubby girl...who was curled up in the center.

"Alice?"

The girl glanced up. Her face, her hands, just as gray as the moss. Eyes just as black as those trees. "Are you here to taunt me too? To tell me how fat I am? How ugly and revolting?"

"What? Of course not! I heard you and—"

"Because I've heard it all! Slow and fat. I knew they were making fun of me. Laughing that all I was good for was to carry the water and their stupid bag of Snickers."

A sob broke out. Wracked through her body.

The branches lowered. Bent and twisted. They reached for Alice.

"They thought it'd be funny if I ate the whole thing myself. Well, I didn't! I didn't."

A gnarled, twisted, and forked branch passed right into Alice— then faded, as if they were becoming one.

"Alice, listen to me." Kate took a step forward. Boots crushed the dry, parched earth and moss. "There's nothing wrong with you."

Kate pushed through the dense branches to reach Alice. Snapped and broke any that were dumb enough to touch her.

"There's nothing wrong with you, just like there's nothing wrong with me."

Alice lifted her tear-streaked face. Gazed at Kate as if she wasn't sure if Kate was real. She blinked. Once. Then twice. "What...what do you mean?"

"Who cares if we're different? Who cares if we don't look like the Heathers or the popular girls of the world? Who cares if we're a little overweight or just have stupid-ass, crazy good-hearing that's just seriously not natural?"

A clawed-looking tree limb grasped Kate's arm.

She yanked herself free. Spun.

Snapped it, clean in two.

Kate reached Alice. Stood over her, hands on her hips and mad as all hell. "Me? I'm done caring because if I didn't have these weird ears and weird hearing I would never have found you."

"You...you aren't a memory."

"No. But I am really, really glad to meet you." Kate knelt beside Alice. Held out her hand. "I'm Kate."

Alice, who was still on the ground, blinked up at Kate as if this whole thing was a really cruel joke. But a pink tinge was coming to her face.

Kate really, really hoped that it was hope. They'd need some to actually get out of this creepy-ass forest.

Alice reached up. Took Kate's hand. A hand that was way, way to cold to be natural.

"How did you found me?" Alice asked.

"I heard you."

Alice looked like she didn't believe her. That was fine too.

And, for the first time ever, it was.

"Do you really think we can get out of here?" Alice asked.

"Absolutely."

How exactly they'd get out, well, that was another matter. One not worth voicing right at this moment.

"Can you stand?"

Alice, who'd been out here for a few days, actually looked pretty good. Other than the practically-no-color part. Even her shirt, pants, and jacket had gone gray. As if they were the first things to get bleached of life.

Kate swallowed. Didn't want to think about what would have happened if her eagle hadn't led her to Alice....

"That's right," Kate whispered.

"What is?"

"We just might have some help after all."

Kate gazed into those dark trees with those branches—now starting to sway and bend their way. Clearly none to happy about losing their next meal.

"Eagle?"

Wings arched out. Stretching. Flapping.

But something else answered as well.

Chittering. Creeping.

Kate yanked Alice upright. "Can you run?"

"Yes, I...I'm not very fast. My friends weren't lying about that. About my weight."

"Good. But I won't leave you. No matter what happens."

Kate tightened her grip on Alice. Swung her backpack over her shoulder, but ready to ditch it—or throw it—at any of the creepy crawlers that even thought about coming after them.

"That guy at the visitor center said we should stay put. If we ever got lost."

"That's probably great advice. Normally. But I'm not about to let this stupid forest, or its stupid fog, take me. Or you."

Out of the corner of her eye, she glimpsed dark shapes moving. Slithering towards them.

Shadows.

Wings lurched from a branch. Her eagle? He was above her, this time, definitely above her. She heard him take flight and out...out of this fog?

The hell with it. Freak or not, she was out of here.

Together.

"Come on! This way." Kate pulled Alice after her.

"But how do you know?"

"I just do."

And she did. She could hear.

Kate pushed her sluggish feet against the thick, dim, and gray moss. Running and pulling Alice with her.

Followed after her eagle, heard his wings high above, as if he were leading the way out of this gray, shady world.

She kept her eyes narrowed. Strained to see through the fog... ducked as a branch came into view.

Nearly tripped over another root.

Kate's breath puffed out. Harder this time to breathe. Colder, too. Like the fog, this forest, someone, some conscious, was doing every-thing to hold them, to mar them down right here, right to this place....

The ground sloped down.

She hadn't seen. The fog, that sneaky, cheating fog, had hidden it from her.

Both she and Alice tumbled down, down. Slid. Fell. Kate's legs slammed hard into the dry, parched ground. She felt the impact roll through her limbs. Alice nearly went down again, but Kate yanked her upright.

They had to keep going.

Moist, rain-touched air drifted to her. Slim snatches of green pierced through the gray.

Nearly out.

But the shadows kept up with them. Darted in and out from the slim, dead trunks of trees. Clawed at them. Taking bits and pieces of them. Life, memory, hope. They didn't let up either. The shadows, and whoever had sent them, trying desperately to convince her that she didn't belong, would never belong in that world with its beautiful and totally normal people.

Kate just ran. Just followed the fluttering, beating of eagle's wings, guiding her. For the first time, trusting in who she was.

Not normal, but different.

Even if her mom had lied. Had kept the truth—whatever it was—from her. But no more. She was done with the lies, done with the pretending. Now, now she wanted answers. After they got out of here alive, that was.

The wind from their running pushed the hair back from Kate's face.

From her ears.

She saw Alice glance up at her. Saw that slight widening of her eyes, which Kate was glad to see were turning to a starling blue. And still, she couldn't help but remember Heather that day, when Heather had confronted Kate and she'd been so very, very angry. And afraid.

As if sensing her thoughts, Alice squeezed Kate's hand. She whispered, a bare breath passing from her lips, "Thank you. However you found me, thank you."

"You're welcome."

Kate's ears, with their slight tip at the ends. Not fully curved, not like most people. It was just a slight difference, but a difference.

And it didn't matter. Whoever Kate was, whatever she was, didn't matter. Being different would get them both home.

It did.

Together, they got back to her mom, Alice's friends, and the search-and-rescue guys. And the one with the single eye, the color that couldn't seem to stick, hazel and blue and then yellow—Kate really just didn't care, she practically flung Alice into his arms. But for a moment, so fast and brief, she swore she thought he grinned at her. A grin that was both joyful and knowing. As if he'd known exactly where they'd been...a world of shadows and mist. She wanted to ask, opened her mouth to demand what the hell was going on—shadow world? Deadly, life-sucking mist?—but then, he and Alice were gone. Simply whisked back to the visitor's center in a throng of over-stuffed jackets and protective rescue workers. Probably an IV and bags of fluids and electrolytes for Alice. And, Kate sincerely hoped, some real food for surviving on her own for so long.

Of course, this left Kate and her mom together.

Alone.

Kate's chest was heaving, as if her lungs couldn't pull enough breath in...the breath that was oh-so-wonderfully warm and filled with life and colors! Sweat dotted her forehead, sliding down, but somehow still freezing cold. She didn't care. She'd made it out of there, and, if she were honest, came out with more than she'd had before.

She reached up, touched the tip of her ear. Yes, she was different, but maybe...maybe different wasn't all that bad. Maybe.

Her mom stood there, her whole body shaking as if she were the one who'd come running out of the shadowy, mist world.

"You came back." Her mom's voice was barely a whisper. "You made it back."

"I did."

"Niflheim. How did this...how can it be?"

Her mom took another shaking breath. Tears slid from her eyes, and they didn't stop, even as she pulled Kate into her arms. In fact, it felt as if her mom was more scared now than when Kate and Alice had stumbled out of the fog.

Kate pulled back slightly. Met her mother's eyes. "You know where I was? You know what happened to me?"

Her mom closed her eyes.

"I want the truth now. No more lies. No more pretending."

"I...I can't."

Kate almost pulled away, almost ran right back into that forest to demand answers from someone, even if it was only a creepy-ass forest, but...her mom held her there, as if she knew.

"But," her mom said, "I will take you to someone who can, who...might know."

"Who?"

"Your grandmother."

Kate didn't bother to ask questions, knew damn well her mom wasn't going to answer them. Hell, she knew only a handful's worth about Grandma as it was, because Mom refused to speak of her. But, if this was the first step to Kate finding answers, to understanding where she'd just come from and what had just happened, she'd take it.

"When?" Kate asked.

"Soon. I promise."

Kate gazed once more into the forest, which now felt innocent, with just the usual mist from the rains that clung to the air, dripping down off pines and branches. That moist wetness of leaves and dirt and life.

All totally normal.

Except for Kate...and what she'd just seen, lived through, and then...found her way out of again.

Normal, but different. The question was: Would she accept it or keep fighting, keep pretending, just like her mom was still trying, desperately, to do?

Honestly, she didn't know.

She just wished she could go back to who she was, before Heather outed her to the whole school, before coming here, and yet...at the same time, she knew she couldn't. Never again. Because what had happened to her, to Alice, in that shadow world—it was real. And someone, for some reason, had been trying to kill her.

Or get her to wake up.

Kate wrapped her arms around her middle and shivered.

HIDDEN IN TRUTH

An Elven Heritage Short Story

HIDDEN IN TRUTH

The freezing-chill Montana air zipped into the closet-sized grocery store as soon as the glass doors, moving at about the pace of a snail—maybe two snails racing neck-to-neck—creaked opened, and then closed again. All those canned vegetables and peaches, piled almost to that stained ceiling, didn't seem to mind the cold. Sure they rattled a bit, just 'cause they were piled so high, vaguely threatening to toppling over with a loud crash, but that was all.

Nothing at all like Kate, standing there, her poor hands whiter than they'd ever been in her life, clutching her Cap'n Crunch cereal box and truly considering just abandoning it and heading back to Grandma's behemoth truck, a truck that barely ran, but hey, at least it still had heat.

'Cause her simple long-sleeved shirt? Yeah, it wasn't exactly the best protection against late-spring winds, apparently.

Nor were her jeans, especially the holes ripped in her knees.

She was shaking from head to toe, so cold that she'd lost her sense of smell about five seconds stepping outside the truck, and wondering why stubbornness ran in her gene pool...and caused her to leave her perfectly good, new sweater in the truck. Okay, the chances of the sweater actually being warm, and you know, *useful*, were pretty darn slim. But hey, it was a nice shade of pink that really went with her tone, and at least it gave the hope that she might, you know, stay warm.

Not that she'd been prepared for this weather. The cold, how it lingered in the air even after the sun finally decided to creep up into the sky, how it settled in your bones and just kinda hung about all day long.

Seriously, how *could* she have prepared when her mom had literally sprang from nowhere: Oh boy! Let's go visit Montana and meet the grandmother you'd had never met in your life.

(The same grandmother, by the way, that her mom had sworn she was never, ever gonna meet.)

All of which would have been fine, or mostly fine, except for the really cold part, if she wasn't standing there in the cereal aisle, the giant-sized (and camping-sized) boxes of Golden Grahams and Lucky Charms and the nasty, fake-wheat-healthy stuff towering over her, staring at her, practically *begging* that she take it and liberate it from this dusty hole of a grocery store (where they'd probably been parked on the shelves for at least three years). The staring, begging cereal, she could handle.

The boy staring at *her*, not so much.

Kate ducked behind the Cap'n Crunch cereal box. Her loose blond hair fell over her shoulders, the tangles getting worse even as she attempted some kind of secret-spy move. Which was, honestly, really dumb, and if she'd had a half second to think instead of react, she would have calmly set the cereal down, turned, and walked away. But she was not a calm person. She was a person used to hiding, a person forced to hide.

She barely kept from reaching up. From touching that slight tip to her ears.

Different. Always, different.

Just as she'd always hid who she was, something she didn't understand and had no hope of understanding because her mother had refused to speak of it. Even now. Even after what happened a month ago when she and her mom went hiking around Mount Rainier.

Kate had always hidden who she was, that slight difference that followed her no matter where she went, no matter who she met, what county or what state, it didn't matter. She was different and there was nothing, nothing at all, try as she (and her mom) might, would ever change that.

Not to mention how impossible it was to hide the deep blush that had brightened instantly when she saw the boy, standing just down the aisle from her (near the Lucky Charms), and those gray eyes of his instantly zeroing in on her.

And then, not leaving.

Which meant she looked like a blinking red stop sign. The kind found in those upscale housing communities where people needed actual lights because they were "special" and they couldn't just, you know, *read* a stupid sign.

Hoping like hell the boy had moved on, Kate peered around her cereal box.

Nope. Still there.

Still staring, too.

Tall, lanky body, probably around her age—seventeen, maybe eighteen—holey jeans and all. His head was cocked to the side, a small smile tugging at his lips, and...joy practically dancing in his eyes.

All of that would have been kinda fine, if not for the way her heart pounded and her face heated. And there was this pull, a pull from some place deep down, some place she was afraid to even acknowledge was there, that it existed. Because she suddenly remembered that day in the woods, the hike with her mom that had started her on this cold-ass journey to Montana. How Kate had found herself lost in this misty, freezing-cold world. A world of no colors.

Kate gripped the cereal box harder, her fingers bending the cardboard.

She would not remember. She would *not* think about that day.

Instead, she focused on the boy and looked behind her, thinking for sure he was looking at someone else, 'cause that was the *only* time she got smiles like that...

Except there was no one.

Besides Grandma, anyway. Grandma in her floral dress that came to her shins, who didn't even attempt to hide the mud-splattered hiking boots. She didn't have a coat or a sweater on either, but if she was cold, she didn't show it in the slightest. Certainly not in the way she grinned and went about with that booming voice of her, talking so loud the people in the next county could hear.

Now, sure, boys were common in grocery stores, even this one, Lighthome Groceries, which was about the size of a bathroom and still managed to stock floor-to-ceiling what the big chains carried.

Generally, though, boys moved on and did what they came for. Buying Cheetos, hot dogs, beer (though this one certainly didn't like he hit the twenty-one age yet, even the fake-ID age).

But he was still standing there, hands tucked in his pockets, just... watching her.

Which he'd been doing the moment she'd walked in those doors.

Her grandmother, whom she'd only just met for the first time, like, *ever*, and who was making Kate seriously, seriously reconsider her mom's sanity about coming to this back-end-of-nowhere town at the furthest little tip of Montana. You've probably heard of Glacier National Park and Whitefish, a big-old fancy ski resort for the rich (and people who saved big time for vacations).

But Lighthome? Probably not.

Lighthome, a town of like, fifty, that even Google had never heard of before. Seriously. It was that small. But hey, they had a grocery store, at least.

Finally tired of being stared at (and tired of looking like an idiot just standing there and blushing), Kate turned to her grandmother. "Who's that?"

Okay, fine...she *might* still be hiding behind the cereal box.

Grandma, on the other hand, didn't bother hiding anything. Not her obvious stare and certainly not her booming voice.

"Who?"

Grandma wheeled around, floral dress flapping about her scarred knees, boots leaving giant clumps of dried-up mud on the equally stained checkered floor.

"That?" Grandma asked. "That's a boy. I thought you could tell the difference?"

Kate groaned and ducked behind the cereal box so the boy—yes, he *was* a boy—couldn't see her beet-red face. No wonder her mother left as soon as she was old enough: Kate's grandmother was seriously unbelievable.

And this, *this* was the only person who could give her answers about her heritage? Help her fill in the missing pieces of why she was so different, so unusual? What was Mom thinking? This woman was *nuts*!

"Grandma. Stop. Looking. At. Him."

"Why? If you didn't want me to look, you shouldn't have asked me to look at him." Grandma plucked the cereal box out of Kate's hand and put it back on the shelf. "You don't want to eat that. It'll make your teeth rot."

Having lost her shelter, Kate had no choice but to face the boy. Sure, she could have dived behind Grandma, but that really was a bit childish.

Kate's face reddened even more.

Hiding behind a cereal box, however, was not.

The boy, she noticed—and again, *boy* was a relative term here—had his own cereal box in hand. But unlike Kate, he wasn't pretending like Kate was.

Nope. He was still staring right at her. Not hiding it one bit. Not a one.

The boy smiled. The freckles on his cheeks stood out even more, and his eyes were so very gray.

Kate spun around. She didn't smile back.

He was probably laughing at Grandma. As far as Kate was concerned, everyone laughed at Grandma. How could they not? No one wore brightly colored floral dresses, especially when there was snow on the ground. Spring, her mother said, didn't come to the north very often and when it did, it was often late and still cold. Here they were, even a few days into June, and Kate still felt like she needed a sweater standing in full sunlight.

Lighthome was the place her mother had run away from the second she could, really not much older than Kate, and hadn't looked back. Until this week. Or, really, until they'd gone hiking in Washington, at Mount Rainier, and Kate had a strange, not-fun experience involving shadows and mists that were trying really, really hard to eat her.

And the girl Kate had found, and brought home: Alice.

Kate closed her eyes, fighting really hard to *not* remember. It had been her...strangeness...that had found Alice and gotten them back safely again. Kate had thought she'd come to terms with, you know, being different. Weird. But school and a former best friend pretty much refused to let that newfound belief stay safe, and she had found herself hiding again.

What if...what if that the shadowy mist world hadn't actually been real? Hadn't actually happened?

Part of her, well, it was okay with believing that.

Her mom, though, had made a promise and she wasn't about to let Kate live in Pretendville. She'd reached out to Grandma, a woman Kate had never met, and so...here they were. A place with a single grocery store, no traffic lights, and signs strung up along the roads that said "Moose Crossing."

To say the least, this place (and Grandma) were *not* what Kate had expected.

What a way to celebrate her birthday, all seventeen years of being weird.

Grandma was currently putting back all the cereal boxes back, and Kate huffed and snagged the last one before the old hag found its proper place in the aisle.

"Honestly, Kate, there's nothing but sugar in that box. What you need is a nice whole meal with eggs, vegetables, some good uncured bacon. I've still got the pig Earl helped me slaughter last fall. That, dear, is a real breakfast. Not this."

Grandma poked the box, but Kate wouldn't let go.

"I like the sugar." Kate held the cereal out like a shield.

If she'd known grocery shopping was going to be a nightmare, she never would have come. And to think that boy over there watched the whole damn thing. No wonder her mother had given her *that* look right before Kate had dashed to the car for a short grocery expedition.

And, the boy had probably seen Kate riding in that monster of a truck, too, because really that was just her luck these days.

Kate muffled a groan behind her hand. Just fantastic. Trip over, birthday over, she was just ready to go home.

Grandma sighed, but merely gestured for Kate to put the cereal back in the rickety cart. Only a week, Kate repeated to herself. A week. Then they could leave, go back to her weird, miserable life, and then she'd never have to see her grandmother again or this tiny town with the strange boy...who was *still* staring at her!

Grandma picked up her shawl, shook it as if it'd actually do some good, then peered around Kate.

"Oh, that's the Sky boy, James. I think he likes you; hasn't been able to take his eyes off you since we walked in."

She knew it. He'd seen the behemoth.

"Would you like me to introduce you?" Grandma asked.

"No! I mean, no thank you." The fewer people she met, the easier it would be to forget this place.

Still, she couldn't help sneaking another glance. This time, his smile was accompanied by a small wave. God. She'd never live this down. But then the boy, James, put the cereal back, turning just slightly. Enough for her to see.

Kate's breath caught. Her fingers tightened on the cart.

His ears. They were like hers.

Grandma tried to move the cart and when she couldn't 'cause Kate was still standing in the way, harrumphed at Kate

"Ah, I *see*. A good lad. You'd like him. Might have a few things in common, you know, between you two."

No. They didn't. Couldn't.

Kate lifted her hand. She didn't want to; couldn't stop herself. She brushed back her sandy-blond hair and touched her ear, fingers trailing upwards towards the tip, and froze. She closed her eyes, felt the slight tip. Different from the usual nicely curved ears, the tiniest marker that she was different.

Tiny, but gigantic at the same time. A difference everyone seemed to notice. Like her former friends at school and everyone else she'd ever met. Especially when she started overhearing conversations from a distance, which was not normal.

James had noticed. That was why he'd stared at her, but for a different reason.

Could he be like her? Truly?

Kate let her hand drop. Was this why her grandma had wanted to take her shopping? Had she known? Had she arranged it? Kate had no idea. She didn't know this woman. All she knew was what her mother told her, and that wasn't much. And what she did say over the years weren't nice, either. Which Kate was seeing firsthand for herself.

Grandma was hitting in that "crazy" territory for sure. Like, look at that truck!

Kate grabbed yet *another* Cap'n Crunch box from the shelf and tossed it into the cart. She glared at Grandma, daring her to say anything.

"What else is on your list?"

Grandma sighed and, with a small shake of her head, pulled out the cramped, handwritten list. Kate practically snatched it from her. She needed something to do; anything to get that boy and his ears out of her head.

Her mother was wrong. They shouldn't have come. There couldn't be answers here for Kate, just...just couldn't be! Just a town full of crazies and weirdoes.

Nothing at all like her.

The rest of their shopping was fairly uneventful. At least, all Kate had to do was ignore Grandma's ramblings. Now the old woman was going on about the foods she wanted to cook for Kate, from home-made apple pie to the roast duck for Kate's birthday dinner. A duck, apparently, Grandma had shot herself.

Kate's stomach swirled at the thought. God, she wanted to go home.

By the time they'd reached the checkout counter, Kate was sure she could survive. Five more minutes and they'd be out the door. Of course, there was the twenty-minute drive just to get to Grandma's house, but the thought of slamming her bedroom door and hiding in her room for the rest of the day improved Kate's mood. A glorious stack of books awaited her.

They just needed to get to the door.

Freedom was short-lived. As soon as the automatic doors zipped into view, James got in line ahead of them.

Grandma at once become friendly with James and the clerk,

someone scrawny with a fuzz of red on his chin, and went into a long, lamenting speech about the recent closure of Sunset Road. Or something else of that nonsense.

Kate, on the other hand, was glaring at the exit.

Her limbs tingled with temptation. She was quiet; she could make it. Grandma was distracted and when she finally glanced back, Kate would simply have vanished.

Her unusual and unwelcome, err...gifts were good for something. Like sneaking off. Except, when she took a step, James was there with that damned smile on his face again.

"You're Kate."

She wanted to smack him. Who did he think he was? He was ruining her chance to escape.

"So?" she asked. "Who are you?"

"James." He held out his hand.

She just stared at it.

Yes, it was silly. She knew that. She was also determined not to blush again. He was, unbelievably, so much more good looking up close, including short blond hair standing out every which way it wanted.

James shook his hand in front of her face, nearly smacking her in the nose.

She pushed him away. "Stop that."

"Well, it's polite to, you know, shake."

"Fine."

She shook. See? She was polite—when she wanted to be, which was not now, seeing as how she was stuck in Lighthome, which should *really* be named Middle-of-Nowhere, and when all she wanted was to go home and forget everything. Especially her being weird. And different.

James's smile didn't change. In fact, it got bigger.

"You are Kate!"

"Do I know you?"

"Nope, but your grandma likes to tell everyone about her granddaughter. I knew it was you."

"And not because I was trying to set your hair on fire with my super-mind powers?"

James's smile wobbled but he held it strong. Kate wouldn't have noticed if she wasn't so freakishly good at seeing details.

"Of course. That and your scowl."

He imitated her. It wasn't funny.

"Ha. Ha." She crossed her arms and moved up in line.

Grandma, unfortunately, took this as the perfect opportunity to introduce everyone properly, which involved more handshaking and a scowl, this time from Grandma, for Kate to stop scowling. So Kate played nice for the ten seconds before the clerk cleared his throat and James paid for his cereal box. Not that James was paying attention. He was still looking at her.

Of course, when he plucked the box off the counter, it gave Kate a full, fairly close-up view of his ears. This time she really and truly did blush, and immediately turned away.

She was right. They were like hers.

James raised his eyebrows in question. Again, she ignored him. At least, she'd thought she had ignored him, until she realized she was flattening her hair to cover her own ears.

That damn smile of his was back and he winked.

Winked!

Kate raised her foot, ready to stomp on his, when Grandma tossed a Snickers candy bar at her. She fumbled to catch it and by the time she recovered, Grandma was ringing up her groceries. Not to mention the poor clerk couldn't put a tomato into the bag without Grandma's careful direction.

James was safely out of Snicker-bar-throwing reach, and with a final wave and smirk, he disappeared out the door.

Good riddance. As far as Kate was concerned, the whole event had been a disaster. She would stay in her room the rest of the trip. She didn't care how many books her mother had promised her, Kate wasn't going to open the door a single crack.

The ride home in the red behemoth was noisy and painful. Grandma seemed to find every pothole and ditch on this side of the mountains. Didn't seem to mind at all, either, but Kate's teeth jarred and clacked together every time. It didn't help that she couldn't get James and his stupid smile out of her head.

It was stupid, and she'd never see him again.

"So? What did you think?" Grandma asked, glancing at Kate, all smiles and being casual.

Too casual. Kate was too good at sniffing out traps.

"About what? The town? The road?"

Her teeth cracked together again.

"Well, of course, you'd never been home before," Grandma said. She was all matter-of-fact, too. "It's quaint and it's home, at least for me. Not your mother. She never did care for Lighthome."

Or Grandma, but Kate didn't say that. That would be rude. Didn't make it any less true, though.

Kate shrugged. "It was okay."

"Spoken like a true teenager," Grandma mumbled. "Your mother said the same things when she was your age, right before she took off."

Kate glanced up. Could she be, possibly, maybe, getting some answers?

"My age? And what happened? Mom won't talk about it."

And neither, apparently, did Grandma.

"I can see why. Hard time it was, for her. And, well, you're as tall as she was anyway, just a year shy, though."

Grandma didn't meet Kate's eyes, suddenly very concerned about the bumpy road she'd been rodeo-ing on for the last ten minutes.

"Actually," Grandma said, "I wanted to know what you thought of James. You and he probably have a lot in common."

"We don't."

"How do you know?"

"How do you know we do?"

Kate's heart pounded and couldn't help the feeling, as much as she wanted to. She remembered his ears, remembered, too, the feel of hers as she traced the small tip. Just like his.

She felt her face heat and hated herself for it.

Grandma gave her a pointed look and Kate turned a way. Damn it. Her grandmother had *not* just looked at her ears.

"Your mother hasn't told you much about your heritage, and I respect her," Grandma said. "You're her child and it's her right. But there are some things that can't...well, can't stay buried. Specially when the greater world won't let you."

"What does that mean?"

"Your mom tried running. Didn't work out so well for her. Or you."

Kate dug her nails into her jeans. This time when Grandma found a nasty bump, she welcomed it.

"There's nothing special about me," Kate said. "I'm perfectly normal."

Grandma just nodded and didn't say anything the rest of the drive. In fact, it was the first time since Kate had walked into Grandma's shabby, brightly colored home that she'd stopped talking.

Even with the bumping and tossing truck, so loud it was about to shake her teeth loose, the silence nagged at her. Mostly because it was trying to draw her own thoughts into places where her thoughts had absolutely no business going.

A magical gift of her grandma's, at least, so claimed her mother. This was why her mother always stated they could not, and never would, visit Grandma. Nothing good would ever come of it.

And yet, here they were.

In this, Kate had to agree. The last thing she wanted was to think about James, his ears, or about the mist and shadow world that had nearly trapped her before she'd found the lost girl, Alice.

No! She was *normal*. A perfectly normal teenager on a required distant family vacation. Not a vacation. That would mean fun. No, this was a visit and nothing more.

Even if there was someone like James here.

By the time they got back to the homestead and Kate pulled back the gate, locking it behind the truck so the cows wouldn't get out, it was nearly dark. The air had a cold bite to it that Kate wasn't comfortable with. Nothing like their small place in Seattle. Plus, it reminded her too much of that *day*, of that hike in Mount Rainier.

Out here, though, there were stars. Back home there was the distant light of buildings and homes and the echo of honking cars and rumbling engines. Here, there were coyotes, and they sang every night.

Grandma turned off the behemoth and the engine died in triumph.

"By the way, I meant to tell you earlier. We're having company for dinner. Tomorrow."

Kate's hand stilled on the door handle. She didn't want to ask. She wanted to be left alone. Like that was going to happen.

Grandma waited, quiet and expectant. For the briefest moment, Kate lost herself in Grandma's eyes, distant and cold, yet something completely familiar. Something she almost ached for.

Almost.

"Tomorrow's my birthday," she said.

"Yes. All the more reason to invite guests over."

"I don't know anyone here."

And if she couldn't spend time with her few friends back home.... The truth was, she didn't have any. Not anymore, anyway. But the very last thing she wanted was to spend her birthday with strangers and distant relatives.

Grandma patted Kate's knee like she was a good dog. "It's important to make new friends."

She didn't like making new friends. Friends and she never seemed to work out.

"Who?" Kate asked.

"James. His mother, too, if she'll come."

Kate jumped out of the truck. The door slamming behind her was more than enough of a reply. For good measure she slammed the porch door as well, waking the two old Labrador Retrievers from their place on the porch swing. Her mother called from the kitchen and Kate caught a whiff of roasting chicken, something they never had at home, before she stomped up the rickety stairs. Loudly.

Of course, she had to hear about her rude behavior later at dinner. Her mother complained, to which Kate simply pushed around her unwanted mashed potatoes with her fork. At least her mom's attitude switched to Grandma when Grandma announced they'd be having guests over tomorrow. Her mom was *so* not happy about that.

They spent the rest of dinner glaring at each other, which was fine by Kate. Neither said anything when she left the table early or when she stomped back up the stairs.

One more week. Then it'd be over. She'd never come back to

Lighthome. And now that she was here, didn't blame her mom one bit for leaving.

Unfortunately, whatever silence holding back her mom and Grandma broke the minute Kate cleaned her plate and left. They didn't even try to be quiet.

Okay, that wasn't quite true.

Kate leaned against her bedroom door. Their voices were clear and distinct. They weren't yelling; in fact, they weren't even talking loudly. She shouldn't be able to hear them.

But, of course, she did.

She was normal. Perfectly normal.

Her mother, however, wasn't helping.

"What did you do?" Her mother snapped. "I brought her here on one condition—one condition—and who do you invite? I can't believe you did this."

"And I can't believe you haven't told her. Does she even know the stories? Does she even have some understanding of who she is?"

"Of course not," her mother said. "She's a regular child, a teenage girl, and I will not let you fill her mind with your fancies and magic faeries."

There was a sharp slap. Kate's eyes snapped opened. She heard the sound, echoing in her mind, heard it as her Grandma smacked her palm onto the table.

She knew, could hear the difference. Grandma hadn't smacked her mother, but the table. With her bare, open palm.

She shouldn't know that. Shouldn't be able to tell from listening through a closed door up a flight of stairs. What was wrong with her?

"Not faeries. Don't even insult them with the name. You should know better."

Kate heard the scrape of her mother's chair as she stood.

"I knew better than to come back," her mom said. "I shouldn't have, and I shouldn't have brought Kate."

"That's not what you said on the phone. Mount Rainier. Her falling into Niflheim. You think you can deny that? Deny that someone was after her?"

Kate's breath caught. She recognized the name; it was what her mom had said when Kate had come running out of that shadow world with Alice.

"You can no more fight the pull than she can," Grandma said. "You know—better than anyone else in our family, *you* know."

A door shut and the conversation died.

Kate breathed. She shouldn't have eavesdropped. She pulled her knees to her chest. Her grandmother was wrong. There was nothing strange about her. She wasn't different and what had happened in...in Niflheim...that wasn't real. She was just lost in the forest and it was scary with lots of mist and shadows. She'd gotten lucky and found Alice.

That was all.

RIGHT?

Still, Kate couldn't help but feel a slight ache in her chest, the same she'd felt earlier when she lost herself in Grandma's eyes.

She pressed a hand on her chest, forcing the feeling away.

It wasn't until later, after she'd turned off the lights and felt herself drifting to sleep, that she remembered it was something she's seen her mother do a thousand times: pressing a hand to her chest, a sorrowful, longing look in her eyes. And a sadness, one that ran so deep Kate could never see how far it went.

Some time in the night, the coyotes woke her.

Kate's eyes snapped open. No. Not coyotes.

A soft tap on the glass of her window. It came again, faster this time.

Kate scrambled up and peered into the dark. Her heart pounded and she barely heard the rap-tap of rocks.

Rocks? Was someone there?

She wrapped the quilt around her and crept to the window, body low. Not even the boards creaked under her weight. She tried not to think about it, tried not to remember how unnatural it was.

Another ping. Her fingers tightened on the quilt.

She had no weapon, although she could scream. Grandma had

more than enough guns downstairs to hold off a zombie apocalypse or something. At least Kate's ultra-quiet abilities meant whoever was outside her window wouldn't know she was awake, and if she needed to sneak away and get Grandma and her guns, she could.

Carefully, making sure the moonlight didn't reveal her, Kate peered over the ledge. Even with the silver of moon, it was still dark. She narrowed her eyes, letting them adjust to the mix of dark and light. Then she saw him.

James.

Kate sprang from her crouched position and nearly flung the windows open. "What do you think you're doing?"

James paused mid-throw and grinned at her. Grinned. How dare he!

"Good morning, Sunshine."

"What. Are. You. Doing. Here?"

Kate wasn't in the mood. First her Grandma, then her mother, and now this.

"You know what? I don't want to know. Forget it. Go away."

She closed the window, careful not to slam it and wake her mother. Thank God Kate's bedroom was on the other side of the house. There was a slight chance her mother wouldn't have heard.

"Come on, Kate." James's voice drifted to her.

He was whispering and still she heard him as if he were standing beside her.

"I didn't mean to wake you." He paused. "Okay, I did, but that was only because you wouldn't talk to me before."

Kate squeezed her eyes shut. This was why she didn't want to talk to him. Because he knew. Damn it, he knew she could still hear him.

"Just give me ten minutes," he said. "If you think I'm wasting your time or you don't like what I have to say, I'll go. Promise."

She didn't know him. She'd met him for five minutes at the grocery store. Except she remembered his ears, the slightly curved point, so like hers.

Kate couldn't help but remember the conversation between her mother and Grandma.

Faeries.

Ridiculous.

"Kate." It was James. He was still down there, waiting. "Aren't you curious?"

"No."

"Yes, you are."

Kate jumped, startled. He'd heard her?

She swallowed, unable to think straight. He had heard her. She peered through the window, but didn't open it.

"See? You're curious. Five minutes. That's all."

It was wrong and stupid and she should just go back to bed. After telling her mother about the boy tossing rocks at her window.

Kate tossed the quilt down and slipped on her slippers and a warm coat. Then she crept down the stairs.

It was harder than she'd expected. Her mother's hearing was good, but Kate had learned to gauge just how well since she was a little girl. Still. The dogs were a piece of cake, but there was Grandma to consider.

She made it outside without incident, or else they'd let her go and pretended they hadn't heard. It was easier to not think about that. Much easier to be mad at James; after all, he was the one who'd woken her up.

James didn't seem surprised when she rounded the corner. In fact, his lopsided grin grew wider. She grabbed his arm and dragged him away from the house.

"Hey! Watch the shirt. You don't need to be grabby."

"I'll grab whenever I want to," Kate growled.

When they were far enough from the house that Kate was sure her mother couldn't hear, she let go. They stood at the boundary, on the edge of the forest and Grandma's home.

The darkness didn't seem so frightening now even though the woods loomed before her. Somehow, being here with James (and being mad at James) made it much easier to deal with.

"Now." She spun and poked him in the chest. "What are you doing here? Why are you throwing rocks at my window? And how in the world did you get out here in the middle of the night?"

James threw up his hands in defense. "Hang on there! I thought you said you didn't want to talk to me."

Another poke. "You woke me up!"

"If I'd had any idea how rough you'd be, I'd have reconsidered."

"Well, then you shouldn't have come."

James smiled. "Yeah, I can see that. I should have known you'd be like your grandma."

Kate reeled back.

James took the opportunity to distance himself from Kate and her poking.

"My grandma? I'm nothing like her."

"Sure you are. Just because you don't know her doesn't mean you're not like her."

It was absurd. Ridiculous. "Fine. But you don't know me either."

Finally, James's smile wobbled. It didn't quite fall. Instead, it felt as if Kate had stumbled into something else, something deeper. Like the joke she'd made at the grocery store about mind-powers.

"I know you." James met her gaze. He didn't look away. "I've known you my whole life."

She wanted to look away. She wanted to laugh and toss his silly comments to the wind because they were silly. She didn't do any of that.

"Five minutes," Kate said. "Five minutes doesn't quite equal your whole life."

"It was more than five minutes."

The ache in her chest spread, reaching deeper than it ever had before. Kate stumbled back. She pressed a hand against the ache, but it didn't stop. It kept going, reaching for something she didn't want to find.

Deeper. Something her mother didn't want Kate to find.

"Kate. Relax. It's okay."

James was there, kneeling on the ground beside her.

Slowly, so she wouldn't run or scream or back away, he reached for her hand. His hands were warm. The ache lessened, not much, but enough where she could breathe, where she could see.

A cloud covered the moon, hiding what little light it had given off. Kate swallowed. She realized it didn't matter. She saw James perfectly fine and he saw her.

"Who are you?" she asked.

No. She shook her head. She didn't want to know. She tried to pull away, but James held her hand in a firm but gentle grip.

"It's okay," he murmured. "I really have known you my whole life, and I would never hurt you."

She believed him. Damn it, she believed both parts of what he said.

"How can you know me?"

He shrugged as if it wasn't a bid deal in the least. "Dreams. A feeling. We've walked through these woods a hundred times in a hundred different lifetimes. It's part of my gift. That's how I knew you."

"Gift?" A shiver caressed down Kate's spine.

James stroked her knuckles with his thumb. She stared at his fingers, and for a moment, neither of them could take their eyes away from their intertwined hands. Then he looked up.

James's eyes glowed in the night, so gray and beautiful her breath caught. Who was this guy?

"I thought you knew. I thought..." He looked away, though he didn't stop stroking her hand.

She had a hard time concentrating on his words.

"I thought that was why your grandma brought you to the store. I thought you knew."

"Well, I don't know."

Good feelings or not, she was getting a little annoyed the way everyone danced around the truth, whatever the hell the truth was.

"So why don't you just tell me?" she asked.

"I can't. I mean, I can't tell you."

"Is this some kind of joke?" Kate jerked her hands away. "You come here, wake me up in the middle of the night. This is like a bad romance or horror movie."

"No! That's not it at all. Unless, unless you think this is a romance?"

"Not very romantic."

She was determined not to blush. It wasn't her fault his hands had to be so rough and soft at the same time. And it wasn't her fault no boy had ever held her hands that way before.

She was just overwhelmed, was all.

"Look," Kate said. "This is crazy. You're wasting my time. You obviously have nothing special you want to show me so I'm just going to go back to bed and you are going to go home."

She'd have to see him tomorrow, but maybe she could pretend she was sick or something. Her mother wouldn't make her hang out with James, not if she knew Kate didn't like him.

Yes. That was exactly what she was going to do.

James, however, didn't seem to know what to do with her. He'd tucked his hands in his pockets and the boyish charm he'd laid on her was gone. Good. It was better this way.

"No. You can't. Please."

"Go home."

Kate turned. She didn't get far.

James darted in front of her. He was so fast. She'd blinked and he was suddenly there in front of her.

"How did you...?"

"Didn't you ever want to know why you were different?"

She shrugged, trying to act like it didn't matter, trying to pretend her heart wasn't beating as quickly as her breath. He was so close.

"I'm a teenager," Kate said. "We all think we're different."

"But you are."

This time she shoved him out of the way. He grabbed her hands even as she stumbled forward, locking her to him.

"What do you want from me?" she asked, voice breaking. "Why won't you leave me alone?"

"Because I can't. Because every time I sleep at night, I see you. Every night you're there, either you or someone like you. Didn't you want to know why you could hear things, things so quiet no one else could hear? Didn't you want to know why whenever you walked through a meadow, the world stopped? As if the animals there were waiting just for you?"

"Why won't you just tell me?" Kate was shaking now. She tried to pull away but James held tight. "Why won't you or my mom or Grandma just tell me? Forget this cryptic bullshit and tell me."

James pressed his head against hers. She didn't want to think about how his presence comforted her, how her shaking slowly subsided.

"Because you wouldn't believe the stories. Your mother made sure you didn't believe."

"Believe in what?"

She could barely get the words out and even as she did, they were so low, so quiet. He heard her, though. She knew he could.

"Believe in elves," he said.

Kate jerked her head up, nearly smashing James's forehead. He'd been ready for her shock, however, and safely pulled away.

"See?" His smile, no longer joyful, was sad. "You don't believe."

The porch light switched on and the door banged opened. "That's enough, Kate," her mother called. "Get inside."

Of course her mother knew. She'd probably heard the whole thing.

"Well," Kate said, "she was right. There's no such things as elves."

She stepped away and James let her. But his eyes pleaded with her to understand, to believe, to trust. She wanted to press her hand into her chest, to push the ache away until it never came back. She didn't, though.

"They're fairy tales," she said.

"They're real."

Kate shook her head. She'd given him his chance. Ache or no ache, she was going to bed and putting this whole mess behind her. That was exactly what her mother intended for her.

"Katherine Silver. Get in this house."

"I'm coming." She brushed past James. "Good night."

And because he looked so sad, because he'd stirred something she hadn't even known was there, she touched his shoulder. It was a light touch, but more intimate than she'd ever touched a boy before.

A shiver shot through her.

His eyes met hers. Held hers.

He changed before her...no...not quite changed, but adjusted. Shifted. His features shimmered, as if they weren't quite solid, but then James was back.

No. Not back. Different now. Older, sadder. Much, much taller. Long brown hair tied at the base of his neck and his eyes, so piercing in the night.

James lifted her hand to his lips. His kiss rocked through her, and she rocked back. Gasped.

A tiny smile quirked at his lips. "Good night, Kátheryn Silverstar. The journey may be long, but by the time you return, I shall still be here. Waiting."

Kate wrenched her hand free. She stumbled.

James grabbed her before she could fall. The long hair was gone, as well as the older features and the prominent, very pointed ears.

"Kate!" Her mother called, this time more with concern than anger.

Kate didn't care. She couldn't take her eyes off James.

"Who? What?"

James's worry changed to triumph. Joy, pure joy, brightened in his eyes. He carefully helped her to her feet.

"I told you already," he said. "We've met a hundred times."

That wasn't an answer. Not after what she'd just seen or what she felt.

She shoved him away from her. "I'm tired of playing games. Both of you!"

Kate rounded on her mother, who was racing down the stairs.

Her mother froze. "Katherine, don't believe anything this boy says. There is nothing wrong with you."

"At least I'm not the one lying through my teeth," James yelled. "She deserves the truth. It's her life. She deserves to understand why she's different."

"She's not different," her mother hissed. "She's not like you or your mother."

"Or you?" he shot back.

"Enough!" Kate jumped in between them, hands held out. "All I want is answers. No more lies. No more cryptic clues. I want the truth."

"I am your mother and you have no right, young lady, to speak to me this way."

"Fine." Kate put her hands on her hips. "Then tell me why I just saw James transform into an older man with long dark hair and pointed ears. Tell me why I can hear and see better than anyone else my age.

Explain to me what happened that day on the hike, when I came out with Alice and that, that place...*Niflheim*."

"Niflheim isn't real," her mom said. "It doesn't exist."

James stepped in. "It does and you know it. Someone sent it to capture her and she wasn't prepared. You *know* what could have happened and *you* couldn't go in and save her. Not from the shadow world."

Her mother, she went pale. Completely and totally white.

And Kate didn't care. Not anymore.

It was true, all of it. And in her heart, she'd known it. As much as she'd tried to deny it, tried to pretend it hadn't happened, that it wasn't her hearing that had found Alice and got them out again, she couldn't lie to herself. Not anymore.

Tears pricked at the corners of her eyes. She was confused and lost and here were the people who had the answers. Her *mother* had the answers.

"Tell me," Kate whispered, "why I make hardly a sound when I walk. Tell me, Mom, and I'll go inside."

Her mother didn't move. Eyes wide, she shook her head. "I will not, not ever tell you. I don't care how many times you ask or often your grandmother begs, I will not speak of them."

"Who?" Kate pleaded.

Her mother didn't answer.

James did.

"The elves. Our ancestors."

At the very word "elves," her mother huffed. Kate was prepared, ready for the lashing she knew was coming. It didn't matter that she didn't deserve it or that she deserved to know.

Her mother had, and always would be, completely irrational when it came to family and history. For the first time, Kate caught a glimpse of why her mother was this way, though she still didn't understand.

The porch door creaked open, then snapped closed again as Grandma joined them. Why not?

Apparently no one slept up here.

"You will not tell her." Grandma wrapped her hideous shawl around her shoulders. "You've made your point clear on this issue, but that doesn't change a thing. She deserves the truth, just as you did at her age."

"Just because you have stories," her mother said, "doesn't make those stories true."

"No." Grandma nodded. "But these are truth. You have seen the truth in them, just as James has and now, just as Kate has."

Kate stepped forward. She didn't want to, couldn't help but feel reluctance straight to her soul. Part of her didn't want to know. That part wanted to stand by her mother, to deny everything.

She took another step.

It would be a lie, though. Just like the life she was now living was somehow a lie. The choice was hers. They were watching her, waiting for an answer. Her choice.

Or was it really a choice?

It was more a matter of truth.

Kate glanced at James. Remembered the feel of his hands brushing her knuckles, remembered the shadow-man and his lips, so similar, so different. Could she live without knowing?

Try as she might, she couldn't forget that kiss and neither could her body. She remembered the rush of heat and then the sadness following close behind.

"You can't go back," her mother warned. "Once you know, it'll be with you forever."

Kate understood that. She looked at her mother and understood. "Was that why you ran away? Was that why we never came here?"

Her mother's lips pinched. "Yes. And after this, I will never come back. I will go back to Billings and wait for you, *wait* for you to change your mind, to realize you were wrong. But I will never allow this to be part of my life."

The words struck Kate. Hard. She staggered back, surprised at the ferocity in her mother, the need to deny so strong she'd deny Kate.

Grandma came forward, shawl dipping to reveal her purple-dotted nightgown. "Enough, Cian. She doesn't have to decide tonight."

Yes, she did. Kate felt it within herself, felt it within the air.

Certainty settled within her. All her life, it had always felt like they'd been running from something. Her mother, always so distant, distracted, and unhappy.

Kate took James's hand and he let her, though he said nothing. She tugged him forward, up towards her mother and then past her. Kate's focus was on her grandmother, the grandmother she'd never known, the grandmother her mother had tried so hard to deny.

The grandmother who could give her the truth.

What Kate did with the truth was for Kate to decide.

"Tell me," she said. "Who am I?"

HIDDEN IN SHADOW

An Elven Heritage Short Story

Kate crossed her arms, the pale pink sweater her mom had bought her rising up her forearms. The sweater barely pushed aside the chill that even now crept in from the early morning, seeping through the closed windows, under the door. Even in early June, at this northernmost tip of Montana, it was still really, really cold, and sweaters (she'd learned quickly) were a necessity.

Even if they didn't happen to be actual, you know, good quality sweaters (and not just the cute kind).

Still, the sweater and the cold were the least of her concerns. Grandma, on the other hand...

Kate glared at her grandmother's back, and that god-awful shawl with too many tassels and fringes that draped from her shoulders. Grandma, who was bent over the stovetop, cooking sausages and doing her wonderful best to ignore Kate.

The sausages sizzled and one gave a small pop.

Kate willed her stomach not to grumble, even though the sausages happened to smell particularly good. As did those sliced heirloom tomatoes, the pineapple-yellow kind that Kate loved so much (which, come to think of it, how had Grandma known about *that*?).

Maybe her mom had mentioned it before she'd hightailed it out of the mountains, though Kate seriously doubted that.

But even with this...this amazing food that, okay, put her Cap'n Crunch cereal to shame, she was still annoyed—like, *really* annoyed. She'd come here for answers, willingly *chosen* to live with this old woman, a grandmother she'd never met in her life before a week ago. Hell, she'd given up the Internet, of all things, and for what?

All to learn one simple (or not-so-simple) truth: who she was.

Kate's heritage...it was a mystery—to her, anyway. Why she was so damn different than every person who walked the planet (okay, *most* people)?

She couldn't help it. She lifted her hand and traced the outline, the shape of her ear. Perfectly normal...except for that slight tip at the end. Hardly noticeable, unless, of course, you were looking. Unless, of course, you also noticed that she had incredibly good hearing, or the way she moved, silent and quiet, at least compared to most people.

All she wanted was answers.

And instead here she was, fighting a grumbling stomach because within two days of her mom packing up and hightailing it out of Lighthome, Montana, she'd learned nothing.

Absolutely nothing.

She'd at least gotten wise to Grandma's tactics. She wasn't eating a thing until she got answers.

"I want the truth," Kate said.

Grandma hummed to herself, acting as if she hadn't heard. Which Kate knew damn well that she had (crazy-good hearing apparently ran in the family), which only made her grumpier.

"Grandma."

"Such an impatient child. No wonder why your mother kept you from this place."

Kate's back straightened. "That's not why and you know it."

"Still." Grandma shrugged as she dished out a sausage for Kate and one for herself. "She was right, at least partly. All these years of keeping the truth from you? The truth isn't something to be taken lightly, or without caution."

The only thing her mother had been "right" about was warning

Kate that if she stayed, she'd regret it. Stayed here. With Grandma. Which, truthfully, she now did.

"Go get your plate. Breakfast is ready."

Kate did not move an inch. Instead, she dug her fingers harder into the soft fabric of her sweater.

If Grandma refused to give her answers, what was the point in staying?

"She was right to keep me away," Kate growled, "because she knew I'd want answers. Answers which I still haven't gotten."

"See? Impatience; that's your problem. Now eat up. Don't want your food to get cold."

Grandma didn't wait for Kate. She grabbed down two plates from the creaky cabinets, hinges as old and rusted as Grandma herself, and served them sausages and then a really, really good helping of sliced tomatoes to go with it.

And no, her mouth was so not watering. Not in the slightest.

Grandma sat down at the table, careful to keep it steady since one side was a bit unbalanced. She also didn't wait for Kate to sit down, and started digging in. As she did, Grandma tucked strands of her lengthy silver hair behind her slightly pointed ears, ears that were pointed like Kate and her mother's. The only other person Kate knew with ears like that was James. No one else.

She used to feel odd, as if she was different—slightly off from everyone else. Now, it annoyed her. She had been totally fine looking slightly different; in fact, was totally over how her last school experience had a former friend completely turn the whole school against her. Really, she could totally go back to that—could live with it, even.

What she wasn't okay with was Grandma keeping secrets.

Grandma's two Labrador Retrievers, Rocky and Jazz, were sitting nice and pretty beside Kate, a hopeful experience in their big brown eyes. Grandma scowled at them, then at Kate.

The dogs weren't dumb. They knew who slipped them small, yummy treats. Certainly not grumpy old Grandma.

It was a small victory, having the dogs favor her over Grandma (even if it was because of food), but it gave Kate the extra bravery she needed. Let's face it. She didn't want to know why she was different (couldn't she have just been born normal?)...but regardless of what she wanted, she had to know. She couldn't walk away from this, couldn't walk away like her mother had—like her mother now wanted Kate to do.

"You gonna eat?" Grandma asked.

"You gonna give me answers?"

She did, however, sit down. And...much to her disappointment, couldn't help her hands from going and cutting into the sausage, the juice and fat the slipping out, nice and clear and white. Damn, did it look good.

"It's been two days," Kate said. "You haven't given me a lot of reasons to stay."

"Yep. Only two days."

"We had a deal."

Kate had thought it simple and straightforward: she would stay with Grandma and, in return, Grandma would tell Kate the truth—the truth about heritage.

Only problem was Grandma wasn't exactly keeping her end of the deal.

Grandma paused mid-bite, green eyes sharp on Kate. "These matters can't be rushed. I told you in the beginning."

"You told me you'd tell me the truth. The only truth you've told me is you have bad knees, bad gas, and a bad temper during the winter," Kate shot back. "That's not a lot of incentive for me to stay."

"Do you want to go back to your mother? She'd be thrilled. Delighted. You can go now."

Grandma waved her fork at the door, sausage still speared, and the dogs followed with their sad faces. "Go and forget about learning anything of your heritage."

"Maybe I will. I'm certainly not getting any answers here. At least Mom has the Internet."

Disgusted and overwhelmed, Kate snatched her plate and tossed the sausage to the dogs. The dogs scrambled to reach the free food. Kate jumped over them and ran out the door.

To hell with Grandma.

She was tired of playing nice, tired of waiting—waiting for what, she had no idea.

The crisp Montana morning took her breath away, cooling some of her anger. Not the kind of early summer she was used to, even during their latest brief encounter in Seattle. Up here, in the high mountains, parked right next to Glacier National Park, it was still cold in the morning even though it was June.

Which, right now, suited her just fine.

Kate stormed into the forest. She'd never heard of it before, but that was one thing Grandma had been upfront and clear on the second Kate decided to stay: stay out of Alfeim Forest. Kate, of course, had ignored her. She'd gone trudging into the woods anyway. Sometimes daily. Always, though, it felt like someone was watching her.

Which, of course, only made her angrier right now.

A darkness. Or, more like a shadow. It seemed to follow her, floating from one tree to the next. Always out of sight, always hiding in the shadows.

Kate shivered and rubbed her arms.

Silent watcher or not, she hoped the walk would clear her head enough so Kate could at least have a civil dinner with Grandma. Still, it didn't change anything.

Kate had made a mistake. She should never have stayed.

She kicked a small rock and it bounced off a pine tree. Stories. She'd stayed for stories and Grandma couldn't even give her those.

Hooves crushed fallen needles and leaves. Far off, but getting closer. Kate knelt, reaching for a nearby stick. Her exceptional, freaky hearing was good for something.

Like people trying to sneak up on her.

Kate pivoted. Her hand tightened on the branch.

James rode on his horse, Eilan. For a brief moment, the James she'd known for the past two weeks, changed. Shifted.

Kate's breath caught. The older James had returned. Tall and elegant, every movement fluid and radiating grace. His pointed ears drew her attention once again, even as the light brightened.

The vision, as quickly as it had come, vanished.

Kate blinked as she tried to control her breathing, tried to recall what being normal felt like.

James sat straight and tall, his posture perfect even though he rode bareback. He was clearly the teenage boy with short blond hair sticking up every which way it wanted. Not the man from her vision.

Kate dropped the branch and straightened, her leg muscles wincing in sympathy. She had no idea how he could stand that.

"Well, it looks like I was right. You could use some cheering up," James said.

Even though he was still some distance away, he'd known she would hear. Kate, however, clamped her mouth shut. No need to point out their unusual differences.

And it certainly wasn't helping her already fantastic mood. Yeah, let's be reminded about the strange oddities Grandma refused to talk about.

Just what Kate needed.

James, however, simply grinned at her. She really hated that grin.

"What are you doing here?"

"A little bird told me you needed some company." Eilan slowed when they reached Kate, not even needing James's direction.

Kate glared at both of them. "I don't need anyone. Certainly not you."

She stomped deeper into Alfeim Forest, but this time she made as much noise as possible. That small defiance helped her feel more... normal. More human.

James, as was customary, completely ignored her. She heard him slide off Eilan and walk after her, Eilan following obediently behind.

At least James didn't try to speak with her. That was one thing he was good for. He knew when to keep his mouth shut and leave her alone. Though that didn't hold completely true, as he was still following her.

She really, really wanted to be alone.

Kate closed her eyes, wishing for James to disappear. Which didn't work.

She sighed, letting her shoulders relax, letting her mind drift. She tried to forget Grandma and James, forget why she'd even come here to the northernmost part of Montana.

It was strange, out here surrounded by trees. Here there was no sounds of cars driving past, only birdsong and the quiet clop of hooves.

Kate stepped over a fallen log without opening her eyes. She knew it was there, could sense its presence.

Another quirk of heritage, a heritage—and a quirk—her Grandma thought unnecessary to explain.

Kate's temper drained away and in its place she felt a distant ache. She wiped a tear with her sleeve, hiding it from James. She wasn't crying.

"Hey. Are you okay?"

"Yes." She made a point not to look at him. She didn't care if it was a dead giveaway. "Can you please go away now?"

"No. You need a friend."

It hurt, hearing him say that. A friend. Kate had had friends, back home where she lived with her mother in Seattle. Or had lived.

She imagined her mother was already packing their things and looking for the next place to drift to. Without Kate. A city, though. Always a city…or what counted for them here in Montana. Her mother mumbled something about Billings a few times.

That was her mom's choice, though.

"I don't need friends," Kate said.

"Liar."

So what? What did she care what he thought? "Look, I just want to be alone right now."

As usual, James ignored her. Sometimes she thought she was talking to herself. "Did you have another fight with your grandmother?"

Kate shrugged. When didn't she fight with Grandma?

James merely sighed. "What is it with your family? First your mother, now you. You don't seem to get along with your grandmother at all."

"It would be fine if she just told me the truth. Instead she keeps all these 'stories' and so-called truths to herself," Kate snapped. "I didn't turn my back on my mother just to let Grandma lie to me."

James and Eilan had caught up with Kate, and Eilan gave her hand a friendly nudge.

"You know, she might have her reasons." James lifted his hands in defense when Kate scowled at him. "Hey! I'm not saying her reasons are right, but maybe if you understood where she was coming from. Maybe she's scared."

"Scared? I'm the one who's not human."

"Sure you are. You're just...different."

Different.

"That doesn't even come close to how I feel right now."

"Okay. How do you feel right now?"

"Besides angry?"

"Yeah. I figured out anger, what else?" James had his cheery smile back on. An infectious smile.

Kate felt herself smiling in return, then quickly caught it and shoved it aside. James's smile widened.

Jerk.

"For starters," Kate said. "I'm scared. I'm confused and frustrated."

"Nothing new. Everyone in my class feels that way right now."

"Yeah, but I bet they can't see quite so well in the dark or easily listen to hushed voices through a closed door and down a flight of stairs," Kate countered.

"True. And neither can they talk to horses."

Kate froze. "Talk to horses? You can do that?"

James halted mid-step and gave her a sheepish look. "Ah, well, you can forget I said that."

"No way!" She darted in front of him. "You can talk to Eilan? Why didn't you tell me?"

Now he was keeping secrets. Just like everyone else. The thought hurt, a lot more than she would have expected.

"Not. Not exactly." He wouldn't meet her eyes.

"You mean Grandma told you not to tell me."

Her temper was back full force. The woods, once comforting, now felt like they were pressing in, like it was some trap and she'd walked right into it. Again.

"You're just like all of them," Kate spat. "I thought I could trust you."

"You can trust me. Come on, Kate, don't go. I meant what I said earlier about being your friend."

Kate glared at him. Eilan nudged James, pushing him forward a step. She met Eilan's dark eyes, sensing the intelligence there, hidden beneath the surface. Waiting. He could hear her. He understood.

Tears filled her eyes. She wasn't about to cry in front of them. Either of them.

"James Sky." Kate lifted her chin, willed herself to hold on a bit longer. To not cry now. "Stay away from me."

She didn't wait for his reply and ran deeper into the woods. This time she didn't fight the tears. The farther she ran, the more they came. Her tears wouldn't stop, so she didn't stop running.

Finally, out of breath and sides heaving, Kate collapsed against an aging ash tree. She didn't know where she was or how far she'd gone. She also really, really didn't care.

"Tomorrow," she aloud, "tomorrow I'm calling my mother. I've had it. I'm done with this, done with their lies. I'm going home."

A true shame. We will be sorry to see you go." A voice echoed around her, so deep that it stole the rest of her breath.

Kate scrambled to her feet. She tripped over a gigantic root—how she tripped was anyone's guess, seeing how it came up to her chest.

She fell, her butt smacking the ground hard. She scanned the area, looking for the old man who'd spoken. She saw no one.

"Who's there?"

No answer.

Heart pounding, Kate pulled herself into a crouch. If she had to, she could run. What had she been thinking, coming out here by herself?

There were crazy people out here. People like her Grandma.

"I have a gun."

She didn't, but that was what her mother said she should say if she was alone. She was really alone now.

Kate peered into the dense forest, trying to distinguish between shadows and lurking shapes, shapes that could be a person intending her harm. She saw no one, but the hairs on the back of her neck stood.

She knew, without a doubt, someone was watching her.

"James? Is that you? I mean it. I don't like playing games."

"James?"

The voice was stronger now, closer. Kate strained, but couldn't pinpoint where the voice came from. It was all around her, like it resonated from the trees.

"I have not seen the lad today, though he should be along shortly enough."

Kate squeaked and whirled around. She'd heard him that time. Right behind her.

No one was there. Only the old—and extremely tall—ash tree. Kate peered into the branches, but spotted only the movement of birds.

James wasn't there, nor anyone else. The branches swayed again, but she didn't feel a breeze. What was going on?

"Who are you? Where are you?"

"Right in front of you, Little Eagle." A branch creaked, bending towards her as if bowing. Then just as slowly, it straightened again.

The tree had moved. It *moved*.

The world blurred and Kate sank to the ground. She didn't care how muddy her jeans got. She'd let Grandma yell later. Right now, she had to figure this out.

She was talking to a tree.

The tree had no face that she could see. In fact, other than a few swaying branches, it was just like any ordinary tree. Except, he was talking to her.

"A tree? I'm talking to a tree?"

"Why yes. Who else in the middle of Alfeim would you speak with?"

"Ah, I'm not sure. This is the first time, you know, I've spoken with an ash tree before."

The tree gave a large sigh as if a wind bowed its trunk. *"It is a great shame. I've forgotten how enjoyable it is to have someone to talk to."*

Kate stood and circled the tree. Yep. It was a true. No old man hid on the other side playing a trick on her.

She couldn't quite figure out if that was a good thing or a bad thing.

Holy crap. She was talking to a tree!

"Grandma, she, uh, forgot to mention this." Among other things. Like, a lot of other things.

"Yes, well, she's not one for sharing, which I don't think is quite right. I'm in need of company too, after all. Not right at all."

Kate had come back around, a little unsteady, though she told herself it was because she had a hard time moving in the mud. Her wobbly legs had nothing, nothing whatsoever, to do with the talking tree.

"Who are you? Do you have a name?"

"The last I can recall, I was called Yig. Yes, Yig shall do nicely. I have not needed a name in some time as few with the gift have visited me. Not even young James has the knack of it."

That's right, she remembered. Yig said he knew James. "How do you know James?"

"How could I not? Every time the boy rides through, he tramples the forest. Hasty, impatient boy. I think, though I'm unsure, all boys are like this."

"I suppose." Her legs still felt weak and since she and Yig weren't going anywhere, she climbed onto one of the three giant roots, the same one she'd tripped over.

"So, who are you exactly?"

Yig tilted his tall crown, as if getting a better look at her. *"I am myself. An ash tree, older than most, older than any I've yet to meet."*

"And there are others like you?"

The thought was a little disconcerting, especially as she'd had to use the ladies restroom in the bushes a few times. Kate tugged her knees closer to her chest, careful not to tip off the root and fall over.

At least she hadn't gone by this tree. Maybe he could give her a map of which bushes to avoid?

"Hmm...there are some, though most have taken root and changed, becoming like other trees in Alfeim. None are like me, though."

Like him? She wanted to ask why he was different, but thought that might be prying a little too much. Maybe Grandma would have heard of Yig?

"I myself was sleeping for some time, but then I felt a change in the wind. I didn't feel quite so sleepy and there were new footsteps in my woods."

He leaned closer, a small branch pointing at her. *"Perhaps it was you."*

"I haven't been here very long." She'd woken up this ancient tree? Kate didn't know how she thought about that.

She was still trying to adjust to the talking tree concept.

Yig sighed. Several leaves floated to the ground. *"And you'll be leaving. I wish you wouldn't. It has been so very long."*

To be fair, she now knew a talking tree; that was a tiny bit more incentive to stay.

"Couldn't you talk to someone else? You said there were others."

He stretched up his branches, reaching for the bright, warm sun. Every branch and joint seemed to creak and pop.

"Ash. There were others, but they've gone now."

Her mouth had gone dry. "Who were they?"

"The light ones."

The elves? The ones Grandma and James hinted at but wouldn't tell her about?

Somehow, Kate managed to take a deep breath and keep from jumping to her feet. She had to stay calm. If she pushed, he might not answer, and she needed answers.

"Who are the light ones?"

"Your kin, of course, though distant kin now."

Her kin. Not her human kin. Kate brushed the tips of her ears, unable to help herself. A thrill raced through her. This could be her chance.

She lowered her hand. For the first time, her ears didn't bring a feeling of loneliness, the knowledge that she was different. Instead, she felt anticipation.

"Would you—would you tell me about them?"

Yig watched her for several moments and Kate did her best not to fidget, to hold still and let him see how desperately she needed to know. And she did. She needed to understand who she was.

"Please."

"It is not my place, but you are too old by far to be without them. Yes, too old, and you've awoken me all on your own without knowing."

Kate inwardly groaned. Great. Another cryptic guide refusing to give her straight answers. What was with these people?

Err...now a tree.

"I asked my grandmother and she won't tell me anything. I even saw James...." Kate's breath caught. Part of her didn't want to remember, and the other part...

Kate blushed.

James had been older, but not just in age. Ancient and distant. The vision was brief, but it had been enough to show her something else was going on, something she didn't understand, but needed to.

Somehow, complaining to a tree felt good. He, at least, had to listen. There wasn't exactly anyone else he could talk to, and he couldn't slam the porch door and stalk around the house.

"Perhaps it is because she's afraid you're not ready."

"I am ready!" Kate leapt to her feet. "I'm tired of her and my mother keeping things from me and if you're going to do it, too, then I'll just leave."

"Peace, Little Eagle, it is merely a thought." He reached out a branch and it caught on her shirt.

Kate crossed her arms and glared. "Tell me why you keep calling me that. Tell me what that means."

Yig seemed to lick his lips, two giant clumps of moss pressing together. Was he irritated with her already?

"It means that you have come to teach. It is the way of the eagle, and the eagle sits quietly inside you."

Yig parted his mossy lips and harrumphed. *"Or perhaps not so quietly. But nonetheless, it is there."*

Kate highly doubted the teaching bit. Especially since the whole reason she'd stayed was so Grandma could teach *her*.

"Grandma said my ancestors were elves. Did you know them?"

He nodded. A small nest, empty of any eggs, dangled from his boughs, a few twigs holding it in place. The image looked so comical, so unreal. Kate couldn't help but touch his rough bark, running her hand down his trunk. He was real.

Grandma said the elves were real.

Hope stirred. So hard and fast, it nearly knocked her off Yig's root seat. "Will you tell? Please?"

"The light ones. This is the name they called themselves and they were the

ones to name the forest 'Alfeim'. A good name. They came from across the veil, traveling through the mists. I do not remember from where, only that it was not here, *but they came and made Alfeim their home."*

In the end, there was little to tell. He didn't remember much. He remembered their voices, like the softest bird songs, and how their presence had brightened the forest. They were fair, with hair the color of moon and sunlight and nightfall. All, he said, shone with light. They were tall with pointed ears, much more pointed than Kate's.

Like James. The James she'd seen in her vision.

"Are they still here?"

It was the one question Kate couldn't get her Grandma to answer, the one she needed to know. Not even James would tell her.

With a slow sadness, he shook his crown. *"A darkness came over the forest and their songs became silent. I have not seen a light one since. Though, it is difficult to say."*

He rested a branch on the place Kate had touched him. As if remembering. As if saddened.

"They have not walked among the trees but their presence still remains. Distant, faint, but here still. Even now."

Kate licked her lips. "Could they be people like me?"

"The light ones'," he said, *"touch on their human kin is faint. All of Alfeim can still feel the light ones, so something of them remains yet."*

"Could I find them? Maybe I could learn more if I do."

Yig pondered this and finally sighed. *"I do not know, Little Eagle. I believe they've gone. Something of them remains, but I do not believe they do."*

"Oh." Her shoulders slumped.

It would have been so much easier if she could have seen an elf for herself, ask him or her a few questions, pull on their ears and make sure they weren't glued on.

Talking trees, however, was a pretty good indication something was going on. Magic, even though she had never believed in magic.

"Well, if they're gone—and it sounds like they left a long time ago —where did I come from? Wouldn't their gift or whatever go away?" She gestured towards her ears. "Unless my ancestors inbred or something."

"Forest wind, no." Yig huffed. *"Nothing of the sort. Though you and your*

kind are nothing like those who came after the light ones, their human-light chil-dren, the gift of magic strong in them already. Not always true and different at times, but strong."

This wasn't helping her understand a thing. "So, you're saying I'm a descendant from a light one, an elf? I don't believe it. Elves aren't real. They don't exist."

"They don't anymore, but they used to." He leaned forward, patting her shoulder with his leaves. They scratched and stuck to her shirt, but he was trying to be nice so she stayed put. *"And even if they don't exist, you still do."*

"Yes, but I don't know who I am. That's why I'm asking." And he couldn't remember anything. Great. The one ancient tree she found had a long-term memory loss.

"I'm tired of being lied to and tired of cryptic answers. Can't you just please tell me?"

Yig leaned back and she felt a deep sadness within him. Now she'd upset him, too. Man, she was really on a roll.

Kate reached out and brushed his trunk. She didn't mean to hurt his feelings. And it wasn't his fault she was so damn frustrated.

"I'm sorry. I'm angry with Grandma. I'm angry with my mom for keeping all this from me."

"It is the way of your kind, and I easily forget. Perhaps...perhaps this is what you shall teach me, Little Eagle?"

He turned his large crown, looking past her. *"And here, the boy comes."*

James? Kate groaned. He couldn't take a hint. Why couldn't he leave her alone?

"Will you return to speak with me?"

"Yes, of course."

Kate peered through the trees and saw the distinct shape of Eilan heading towards them. Could James sense her? Was that one of his odd abilities?

If so, it wasn't one she liked. He always seemed to know where she was. Jerk.

Yig stretched again, this time it was more like a yawn. *"Then I will leave you to the boy. So much excitement, too much for one day. Now hold your promise. I'd like to see you at least once more before you leave."*

Kate turned away from James. Something about Yig, about his words, pulled inside her. She touched his rough bark again. The smell of ripe, sweet bananas drifted around her.

She closed her eyes, willing him to know she'd keep her promise. She would come back. She wanted to come back.

"Thank you," he murmured.

Kate jumped back. He'd heard her. "Yig?"

He was asleep. She could feel him slumbering, could feel the weighty breaths as he exhaled from the roots to the top of his crown. Asleep, but still there. She could feel him.

Kate knew, without a doubt, that if she were to come here years from now, if she decided to throw away this life and who she was, she'd still be able to find him. She could walk blindfolded and know exactly where he was.

Maybe she didn't need that tree map after all.

"Kate!" James slid off Eilan and ran towards her, not even caring that he'd simply dropped the reins.

Kate immediately pressed against the tree, just in case. She had no idea how well-trained Eilan was and she hoped he wouldn't run towards her like James.

She was fairly certain if she got to chose between a talking horse and a tree, she would pick the tree. A tree couldn't step on her toes.

James practically yanked her from her tree's safety and squeezed her against him. Tight.

"James. I can't breathe."

He didn't let go, though he did loosen his hold. "I'm sorry. I thought I'd lost you. I thought you'd run into the woods and got lost."

"Why would you think that?" She managed to wiggle one arm free, but James's grip was tighter than she'd expected. "Calm down. I didn't go that far."

His grip tightened. Only for an instant, but that was all she needed. He'd thought something had happened to her. He wouldn't have thought that. Not if he didn't have a reason.

Kate shoved him away. "What is it? What aren't you telling me?"

"No-nothing. I'm just happy to see you."

"No you're not. You're scared to death." Kate poked him in the chest. "You're pale, your eyes are dilated, and you've known me barely two weeks."

James made some kind of soothing motion at her, but it had the opposite effect. She wanted to dunk him and every person who'd lied to her in the nearest lake.

"I'll leave," Kate said. "I swear I'll leave right now if you don't tell me."

If she couldn't boss Grandma, couldn't make a tree remember, she was damn well going to bully James.

"It can be dangerous out here, for people like us."

She didn't buy it for an instant. "Not for you. You've been coming here for years, you said so yourself."

"Well, yes...."

"And you told me we're descendants from elves. I'm sorry, in my limited knowledge—very limited, thanks to you and Grandma—it seems like the forest would be our home."

"For some of us." He didn't meet her eyes. "Not everyone."

The hair on the back of her neck rose. She told herself it was the wind or maybe Yig waking up, though she knew he was fast asleep. "What do you mean?"

"You're not the first, you know." James dug a toe into the soft dirt. "Your mother didn't fit in, so she left. There have been others like her, and they left the area too. And they had families."

"What does that have to do with me?"

He shrugged, made a big show of patting Eilan and snatching the fallen reins. As if the horse was going to go somewhere. Yeah, right.

"Some of the families came back, you know, like you. They wanted to know who they were."

Just like her. Different. Afraid. Never quite sure why they were different.

Yes, she could imagine others coming back, even staying behind while their mothers continued their lives without them. Why? Because they needed to know, needed to understand.

"You still haven't answered my question. Why are these woods not safe?"

Part of her didn't want to know the answer, didn't want to admit she was deep in the forest and the only person she had for company was James, his horse, and a sleeping tree.

James shook his head, eyes pleading with her to let this go.

She wouldn't. No way in hell.

"Please don't make me say anything."

Kate stepped closer to the tree. She was now even with where Yig was rooted. Still, James said nothing, though his face paled.

Another step. She wasn't leaving without answers.

"Kate. Please. Let's just go back."

"Not until you're honest with me." Her eyes narrowed. "Fine."

Kate turned. She was done with these games. Anger drove her, made the fear diminish, though it was still there.

James was afraid, which meant somewhere within she should at least be wary. She wasn't. Right now she was pissed off.

Kate took off.

Eilan darted in front of her. Kate screamed, jumping back. She stumbled into Yig's trunk, scratching her elbow. James yelled for her. Kate kept screaming because Eilan kept coming closer.

"Kate. Warm winds, Little Eagle." It was Yig's voice, a small whisper in her mind. She felt the trunk warm as if he were reaching out, trying to comfort her. *"You are safe."*

Kate stopped screaming. James rushed over and pulled her into another hug.

"You can't, damn it, Kate! It's too dangerous." They both fell to the ground in a heap.

She was crying. Damn it. Why was she crying?

"Eilan!" James said something, spoke in a language Kate had never heard before. It was beautiful. He said only a single word, too fast for her to hear, but familiar.

Somehow.

Eilan calmed and Kate calmed. She felt so tired all of a sudden, tired and lost and ready to go home. She hugged Yig's trunk, pressed her cheek against the scratchy bark.

She wanted all of them to go away. Go away and leave her alone.

Her mother had been right. She should never have stayed here.

"Kate," James whispered. He tucked a strand of hair behind her ear, fingers slightly shaking.

"Why are you upset? You weren't the one who nearly got trampled by a half-mad horse."

Something flickered in his eyes, gone before Kate could even see what he was trying to hide. "Eilan's not half-mad and he didn't try to trample you. He wanted to stop you."

Kate slowly released Yig and winced when she felt the rough scratches. They stung something fierce. "Well, I wouldn't have fallen if it wasn't for him."

"You might have been lost if it wasn't for him."

She froze. Waited. James waited with her, worry for her disappearing to plain evasiveness. Maybe it was something in the water. Everyone in town seemed to have the knack whenever these strange stories came up.

James's shoulders fell. "You're right. I'm sorry. You wouldn't have run if I told you, and if you didn't run, you wouldn't have gotten hurt."

She crossed her arms over her chest and got comfortable. They weren't leaving until she was satisfied.

"I'll make a deal with you. Tell me about the forest and I promise not to go in by myself." She remembered her promise to Yig. "Not go past this tree by myself."

"Promise?"

She nodded. "If you promise not to sic your horse on me."

"He was only trying to protect you."

"Tell me about the forest and I won't ask why I keep seeing an older vision of you."

James's mouth dropped open.

"I also won't ask about the strange language you just spoke in." Today, anyway. "Yeah, I'm not that stupid. I noticed. So. You gonna tell me or do we have to do this again?"

She was fairly sure neither she, Eilan, James, or Yig wanted a repeat of her attack and subsequent screaming. In fact, she was fairly sure if there were any other talking trees, she'd woken them up. They probably wouldn't be very nice.

"Your grandma's gonna be pissed," James murmured.

They headed back to the house. James wouldn't say anything until he was sure they were leaving the forest.

"It's the forest." James scanned the nearby trees; what he was looking for she had no idea. "It's not safe for those who reject their heritage. Over the years, kids have gotten lost and were never found."

"Come on. That happens in every forest. People do stupid things. They go off trails, get stuck in a storm; they get lost and aren't prepared." Kate didn't see why this should mean she should be afraid, she or anyone else, for that matter, heritage or not.

He shook his head. "You don't understand. We don't get lost. *Ever.* If a hiker went missing, we could find them, even if they'd fallen into the deepest ravine. Kate. We could find them."

She couldn't help but think back to how this adventure all started: her mom's stupid instance on going hiking near Mount Rainier; the lost girl, Alice; the shadow world that had trapped them both...and how it had been Kate, and her hearing, that got them out again. That... and the overhead flapping of wings.

Her breath caught. Could all this really be true?

Of course, there was the talking tree to consider....

Eilan nudged her shoulder from behind and she merely batted him aside. Fear trickled in, but not because of the horse. Though he was much too close for her liking.

"You're saying people like us have a gift? They can find anyone in the forest?"

No wonder James always knew where she was. Great.

"That's right. Anyone, anywhere, any place. It's part of who we are, though some are better than others."

Her stomach tightened. If James could find her anywhere... She glanced backwards, in the direction she'd run. He'd been afraid. Afraid he couldn't find her.

"People who are lost, they really are lost. That's what you're saying?"

"Yeah. Lost. No trace, no sign, no body. And some of us are the best trackers in the world."

Kate rubbed her shoulders, trying to ward off the sudden chill. Eilan was there again and she scooted closer. He was big, tall, and scary, but right now he felt a hell of a lot safer than being alone. His large (very large) size comforted her.

She'd been alone up until she'd met Yig. Then, like a spoiled, unreasonable child, she'd nearly run deeper into the forest.

This wasn't any easier for James. He could barely look at her.

"I don't know why your grandma didn't tell you," he said. "Heck, I don't even know why your mother didn't warn you about the woods."

"She did." In fact, she'd warned Kate several times on the drive over, which of course meant Kate went and did it anyway.

"Yeah, well, if they'd told you the truth, you wouldn't have gone. It's dangerous, but you couldn't have known that." He scowled. "It shouldn't be dangerous, not for you and not for anyone with the heritage."

James told her more, but it wasn't very helpful. They had never seen what took the kids (and who "they" were, Kate couldn't get out of him). The kids simply went into the forest and never came out again. Sometimes, adults were lost, too.

"Most times, people are like your mother. If they survived until adulthood, they learned to stay away. They don't go into the woods." James kicked a small rock. It bounced hard off a tree but it didn't seem to cool his temper. "They may not believe, but they're not stupid, either."

Kate's steps slowed as they neared Grandma's house. She didn't want to go back, especially when James was actually telling her things.

She decided it was best to play fair and hoped if she told him about Yig, he'd keep telling her about their heritage. When Kate had finished her story, it took her a few moments to realize James wasn't following.

She and Eilan paused. James stood in the middle of the trail, mouth open like a fish, blinking at her as if she'd spouted horns or something.

"What's wrong?"

James tried to close his mouth, and made some kind of strangling noise.

"Huh," she mumbled to herself. "I guess Yig was right. Talking to him was a rare gift."

"You don't understand." James caught up with her. "Agh, it makes me so mad your mother didn't tell you anything. Listen. The last people who could talk with trees were the elves themselves, them and their nearest descendants, the first half-elves. But with...with Yig?"

Again, James swallowed. He still looked rather peaky. Maybe he wasn't feeling well?

"That's silly," she said. "So why could *I* talk with him?"

"Don't you understand who he is? A legend from the old tales, from many of them, in fact!"

She just looked at him.

"You don't know, do you?"

"I think we've been over that."

"He's, well, he's the World Tree. Yggdrasil. Roots and branches and all that connected to hundreds of worlds. You've never heard of him before? And yet...you could talk with him?"

She still just looked at him, this time as if she thought he was spinning one big-ass yarn.

The porch door opened, then slammed shut. Grandma stood there, hands on her hips, a slight bulge in her ugly fuchsia apron. Probably a gun.

"Because the kids of our line are special, that's why," Grandma snapped. "And what the hell do you think yer doing? Runnin' out in the woods by yourself. I know your mother told you better."

"Yeah, well, she also told me not to stay here with you. Remember?"

James waved at Grandma. "Good evening, Mrs. Silver."

"Don't 'good evening' me! You should have known better, letting her go off by herself."

James paled. "It wasn't her fault. She didn't know."

But of course, Grandma was determined to pin this on Kate.

Kate gritted her teeth, listening to the tirade, and suddenly realized where her mother got it from. Then she wondered if she got her temper from her mother—who must have put up with the same damn thing.

"Look. The only reason I ran out in the first place was because of you. And surprisingly, I managed to learn something."

Kate stepped forward, all her frustrations, all her pent-up anger rolling to the surface. Damn Grandma and her damn secrets. "James told me about the forest and the missing kids."

Grandma stilled. Her gaze didn't leave Kate. "Did he now? And did he tell you also what happened to your mother?"

"No."

He hadn't said anything about her mother. She wanted to look back, wanted to demand answers from James, but she didn't want him to see how it hurt.

Her mother? Had her mother seen the darkness?

"James," Grandma said, "I think it's past time for you to be getting on home. She won't be going out again. Not tonight, anyway."

Kate didn't hear him leave, barely even felt Eilan's tail as it slapped her shoulder on his way by. None of that mattered. "What happened to my mother?"

Grandma's lips pinched.

The phone rang, but neither moved. The ringing stopped, only to begin a moment later.

"You better get that." Grandma opened the porch door for Kate, shooing the two dogs outside. "It'll be your mother."

Kate literally had to bite her tongue to keep from asking. If Grandma knew, if she was right, it probably had to do with another of her heritage "gifts".

Sure enough, when Kate answered, her mother's shrill voice yelled out of the receiver. Kate held the phone as far from her as possible, which wasn't very far because Grandma had an ancient, corded phone.

At least it was a touch-tone.

A minute passed before her mother's shrill lowered to an acceptable level and Kate forced herself to answer. "Mother. I'm fine. Why are you calling?"

Kate watched as her Grandma kicked off her boots in the mudroom, then put down an old revolver on the kitchen table.

She didn't seem concerned about what had happened—or that Kate's mother was on the phone. Nope. It was back to work, scrubbing dishes and tossing the dogs whichever scraps she didn't want to save.

Grandma saved everything.

"You're not listening to me," her mother said.

"Sorry. I had a busy day."

There was a short pause, and Kate wondered if her mother was trying to figure out how to say whatever it was she wanted to say. They'd never been good at this, mostly because Kate wanted answers to things her mother didn't want to talk about.

Gee, like her heritage. That must also run in the family. She glared at Grandma.

"Why did you go into Alfeim?"

Kate sat up straight. Her mother knew. How?

"How many times have I told you? If you ever listened to me, for once in your life—"

"Mom. How did you know I was in the forest?"

Silence.

"If you want me to listen, you better start being honest with me. You and Grandma both. And if neither of you are going to tell me, fine. Then I'll ask Yig."

Another pause. From her mother, anyway.

A plate slipped from Grandma's fingers. The shatter echoed through the house, followed by Grandma's cursing.

Mom recovered first. "Yig. Who's he?"

"A tree. I met him this afternoon. He was rather nice, very polite. He'd like me to come back and visit with him. James told me he was called the World Tree. Know what that is? Plan on telling me, *Mom*?"

"Put your grandmother on the phone."

"Fine." Kate passed the phone over, stretching the cord as far as it would go.

Grandma took the phone, soapy hands and all. "Don't yell at me. You were the one who didn't tell her the danger. Well, of course I didn't know she could talk to trees. Did you? Is that why you never let her come here?"

Kate leaned against the kitchen counter, arms across her chest, and glared.

"It's not my place to tell her and it's not my story," Grandma snapped. "It's yours. No. You didn't prepare her. Light ones protect us, you never even told me you hadn't given her *any* education, let alone the proper one."

Light ones?

Kate's breath caught. That was the name Yig had given the elves.

Grandma paused, letting her mother speak, but she held a hand over the earpiece, providing just enough distance Kate couldn't hear a thing.

Damn. She pushed away from the counter. "This is getting old. Tell me what's going on or I'm leaving."

Grandma met her eyes and studied her. She gave a curt nod, then interrupted her mother and hung up. "It wasn't my place, but seeing how neglectful your mother's been, I suppose we'll have to amend that rule."

Grandma wiped her hands on a dish towel and tossed it into the sink. "I'd hoped she would least tell you about the forest and her...well, history."

"She told me to stay away."

"But not why."

Grandma's anger filtered away and for a brief moment, Kate saw her grandma, old and tired, though her spark burned bright and true. Still, she was old. She looked it right now.

Kate's stomach fluttered. She couldn't help but fear the answer, the answer she'd forced Grandma to give.

"I need to know. If there's any hope at all of...of this." Kate gestured to the house. "I need to understand."

"You do. It's just that...it's that your mother had said the same thing once."

One of the dogs sauntered over, as if sensing Grandma's sadness, and nudged her hand.

Grandma smiled and gave Jazz a friendly pat, though the sadness was still there. "Your mother needed to understand, when in truth understanding was the last thing she wanted. See, Alfeim has a way of knowing these things, even if I couldn't see the truth for myself. The forest, it knows and it acts. Your mother...I don't know how much James told you, but your mother is lucky to be alive."

Kate wanted to ask how, wanted to demand the answer. She held her tongue. This obviously wasn't easy for Grandma and whatever she was reliving, the memory wasn't easy, either. And the last thing she wanted was for Grandma to close up. And if she was anything like Kate's mother, she would.

Grandma gestured to the front porch and they went outside. The sun was no longer climbing in the sky and the world seemed to dim, bit by bit. Kate hardly noticed. She'd never realized how good her eyesight was until she'd come here, until she looked out into the dark forest.

Her chest tightened, but not in pain as it had done all her life. It had flared when any of her strange heritage gifts manifested herself, like a physical ache telling her something important was missing.

Now, she felt something different. A pull, perhaps? Not an acceptance, but there was something there.

"I know that look. You can feel Alfeim."

Grandma sat on the porch swing, her bones creaking. She really did look old. Nothing like the vibrant and well-aging woman Kate had first seen. She didn't like that, though she hadn't the faintest idea why. It wasn't as if she was starting to like her grandma or something. The woman was too infuriating for that.

"Did Mom feel the forest?"

After a moment, Grandma shook her head. "I don't believe so, though she said otherwise."

"And Alfeim knew?"

"It knew."

Kate sat on the bench. It rocked gently. "What's out there?"

"The trees, the birds, the earthworms." Grandma shrugged. "They are all individual beings, yet one and the same as well. They are the forest and in this forest, something of the old ones remains."

Grandma sighed. "When the elves lived here, their touch went deep into the land, so deep the land still remembers. It doesn't like being lied to."

Kate could easily relate. Being lied to sucked. "What happened to my mother?"

"She went into Alfeim, though only along the edge. Someone...well, he'd convinced her to try, to prove herself to me. Your mom, though, she wasn't a fool and didn't go deep. A fool nonetheless, though. Alfeim knew her heart, and she'd thought herself safe."

Grandma's sadness settled over her again. It was only Kate and Grandma and the memories.

As Grandma spoke, it was as if Kate were there, running alongside Grandma, into the storm searching for her daughter. Rain pelting every which way, pine needles slapping at her arms, her face. Lightning streaking and flaring across the deep black sky. Fear clutched at her, nearly dragging her under. The mud, so thick it nearly trapped her.

"By the time I arrived," Grandma said, "I don't know for sure... Alfeim wouldn't answer me and I couldn't sense it in that moment. Your mother stood there frozen, unable to move, staring at nothing and everything."

Kate leaned closer, desperately needing to know. "But you saw something."

"Her shadow. Your mother's shadow. It was there, it was angry, and it was coming for her. And I did something I never thought I'd do. I defied Alfeim. I wouldn't let the shadow take my daughter, regardless of whether or not she believed. And Alfeim...it let us go. Both of us."

Grandma rubbed her wrinkled, tired face. "But you see...it wasn't Alfeim that attacked, not exactly."

"But, you just said it was the forest?"

"You want simple, Kate, but our world, our stories, are anything but simple. Tell me, did you see a shadow following you today?"

"Yes."

Kate's heart hammered. The shadow had followed; even when she'd met Yig, she'd felt it near.

"I thought it was the forest," she said. "Was that what...was that what attacked Mom?"

"It is, but it is also more."

Grandma folded in on herself, as if losing more of her youth, becoming the old woman she hid so well.

"It was *your* shadow," she said finally. "The part of your spirit tied to their world. The part of you that is still tied to your great elven ancestors. Any descendant once connected to the elves by their bloodline carries that spirit. For some, that connection is weak; for others, it is stronger. And for a select few, well, let's just say they carry a bit more of the elves with them."

"More?"

"Souls reborn." Grandma waved a hand. "Not many, though, are blessed with *that* gift."

In that moment, Kate thought of James, of how his image would... change. Shift. How she would see someone else in him, both one and the same, but different.

"James," she whispered.

Kate knew darn well that Grandma heard, super-awesome hearing and all, but she kept quiet about it. Instead, Grandma focused on the shadow. Kate let her. For some reason, she didn't *want* to know the truth about James.

And why he was so connected to her.

"For those who don't believe," Grandma said, "like your mother, that spirit changes. Because of who we are, because of our heritage, how even now, thousands of years later, we're still connected to their magic, the forest changes that spirit. It becomes a shadow."

"And makes our shadows real?"

"Real enough to be angered. To pull us fully into that world, the world where all the stories are real and just as dangerous. The world of magic and elven descendants, the one that people like your mother *can't* accept."

Grandma closed her eyes, her forehead creased. "I knew the moment you and your mom came to Lighthome, the very moment you crossed into Alfeim."

"How?"

"Alfeim told me."

Kate tried to speak, but couldn't find her voice right away. She'd seen it, seen the forest. The very thing that had attacked her mother and nearly dragged her into its depth had simply...watched Kate.

"What did it tell you?" she asked.

"That my daughter had returned."

Grandma still had her eyes closed. The dogs had come back, sitting there with their best loving expressions. This time they weren't able to reach Grandma. For this, they couldn't comfort her.

Grandma wrapped her shawl tighter around her, knuckles white and wrinkled. She looked so old.

"But I knew it wasn't speaking of your mother."

LATER THAT NIGHT, Kate couldn't sleep. She huddled in her bed, covers drawn tight around her.

She half-wished James would throw rocks at her window. She needed the company. But she was also afraid of opening the window, of looking out into the darkness and meeting the gaze of the forest. A gaze that was on her, even now, watching her through the very same window.

The whole evening had shaken her to her core. And when Kate had asked about Yig, or Yggdrasil, as James had called him, Grandma had gone even more pale. (How that was possible, Kate hadn't a clue.)

Grandma's explanation had been simple...and yet, anything but simple.

"He...he must have come over with them. With the elves. Or maybe he was already here, his roots connecting our worlds through the veil. Which means...that those stories are true. How hadn't we known, after all these years?"

She shook her silvery head.

"And he spoke to you, of all people, Kate. The daughter of one who'd turned away from us and our heritage."

"Yes, but *who* is he?"

Grandma had then told her a little of Norse mythology, how the World Tree connected all worlds, from the one of the gods to some ice world and then of course, the world of men. She'd also mentioned that Yggdrasil's destruction had to do with the end of the world.

"Those, of course," Grandma went on, "*are* just stories. Or they were until you showed up and started talkin' to him. Truth is, we don't know much because the elves aren't around to ask, and what knowledge we did have was lost over the years—war and what-not, disagreements, you name it. But I tell you now, Kate, you keep your knowledge of Yggdrasil to yourself. It's safer for all that way."

The realization, about her shadow, about Yig, had shaken her as much as it had Grandma. And Grandma wasn't the sturdy, everlasting woman Kate had thought she was. Not a rock. That thought frightened Kate as much as Alfeim did.

She didn't want to be left alone, didn't want to be alone with all these questions and uncertainties.

Fear, however, had a strange effect on Kate. When the glowing light of her clock showed 2:00 A.M., another feeling took over.

Anger.

Why should she be scared? She hadn't done anything wrong. Hell, she'd come here to learn.

And this stupid forest had the nerve to watch her? To try and scare her?

No way. Kate wasn't gonna play.

She tossed the covers off her bed, pulled on warm socks, and stormed down the stairs. She paused long enough to grab her boots and jacket, and strode into the night.

This was her choice. Her acceptance.

When Kate reached the edge of Alfeim, when she felt the darkness within, the weight of the forest gazing at her, Kate glared right back. "I'm not my mother. Don't you dare treat me the way you treated her."

Kate took another step, then another. Now she was at the barrier itself. The boundary where her grandmother's land and the forest met.

The darkness pressed closer.

"I'm not my mother, but that doesn't mean I don't believe her. About you. About all this. I'm not believing any of this on faith."

A branch snapped to the right of her. She didn't look. Her heart hammered from fear and anger, both mixing until they were one and the same.

Kate took a deep breath. She might become lost like the others, but she wasn't about to live in fear, wondering when Alfeim would take her.

"I believe you're real. I believe you have a consciousness and that you can hear and understand me."

Something brushed the side of her face. The wind rolled through the trees, rushing past her, creating a wind tunnel so strong she stepped back. She felt something, or someone, all around her.

Kate didn't look. If she did, Alfeim would win. It would have her.

"What I don't know is if this life, this place is right for me. You might not be happy about it, but it wasn't right for my mother."

Kate crossed her arms. "Now. You can make your choice. You can either give me space and let me decide in my own time, or we can have this out right now. Either way, I'm tired and I'm going to bed."

Nothing stirred in front of her, though she still felt the presence... everywhere. All around her, and even, in some ways, inside of her.

This was her choice. Hers and hers alone.

Not her mother's, not Grandma's.

Hers.

Kate breathed in, lifted her chin, and faced Alfeim Forest. Except there was nothing there. She was alone, alone with Grandma's house before her, the dim porch light a shining beacon in the chill night.

Alfeim's weight, its presence, didn't leave her. It didn't stop her either, nor did it make itself known even as she turned around and trudged back to the house. It was watching her, though, as she opened the door and saw Grandma sitting on the stairs, both dogs pressed against her. Grandma's eyes were red and she clutched her quilt to her chest.

"I thought the forest had taken you."

"Not yet, anyway." Kate closed the door. "I said it could, but it didn't."

"Fool, fool child." Grandma closed her eyes. She was shaking, and though Kate wanted to reach out and tell her it was okay, she didn't.

This woman was still a stranger, grandmother or not.

Kate stayed where she was. "I thought it was more stupid to stay away. That's hard to do. It's kind of...big."

"Aye, it is at that. Used to be bigger, too, back in the before times when the elves were its caretakers."

Kate didn't move. "What was it like in those days?"

"It's hard to say. I wasn't alive, and those we could have asked are gone or have forgotten. Alfeim was wilder, happier, I think. The trees liked to talk and any traveler who'd listen would hear a marvelous story or two."

Kate thought back to Yig and wondered if he'd been one of those trees. She thought he might. He did like to talk.

"The stories," Grandma said, "say the trees used to sing. Every night you could hear the singing leaves and branches while the wind picked up the tune and carried it across the mountains. Some say it sounded like wind chimes."

"Have you heard it sing?"

Grandma blinked, as if realizing Kate was standing there and they were having one of those "must-not-speak-of" discussions. Kate thought it best to stay still. Hopefully Grandma would fall back into whatever mood she was in and tell her more.

"Nah," Grandma said. "I'd never heard the singing. Neither did my mother or grandmother. I told you, it was a long time ago. Alfeim has gotten quieter each year. Little by little, its falling asleep. Whatever the elves had done to wake the trees is fading. Or maybe it's the trees who are fading."

"And new trees," Kate whispered. "Young trees who may have never met the elves."

Trees that, in a way, were not much different than her. Born with strange or slightly unique gifts and yet having no concept or context for what it even meant.

Grandma stroked her chin and Kate relaxed. Grandma's hand was steady now. The danger had passed.

If Grandma wasn't worried about the forest, it meant Kate really didn't have anything to worry about. At least for now.

Later, after Kate had finally coaxed Grandma to bed—after promising she wasn't going into Alfeim—Kate lay in her bed. As she drifted to sleep, exhaustion and dreams taking hold, she thought, in the distance, she heard wind chimes.

HIDDEN IN FIRE

An Elven Heritage Short Story

HIDDEN IN FIRE

The thick layer of pine trees huddled so close together that the night's shadows seemed to blend from one to the other, never-ending, always continuing. A chill breeze rustled through the branches, the pine needles swaying and almost whispering, like a quiet song that you could almost hear, almost understand.

Or, maybe, that was just her.

Kate moved easily through Alfeim Forest. The fallen, dried-up leaves crunching under her tennis shoes as she walked. Not silent, not like her grandmother would be or even James if they were the ones sneaking through the forest at night.

Kate, though, Kate was an entirely different story.

She shivered, the pale pink sweater her mom had gotten her doing absolutely nothing to ward off the end-of-spring chill, a chill that didn't seem to want to let go regardless of the fact that they were straight-up hitting early July. Up here, in the northernmost tip of Montana, just a stone's throw from Glacier National Park (not that she'd been there yet, herself), spring was short and laughable, especially on the whole "warming up" factor. Summer, she'd been warned, was hot as hell. At least during the day. Night, though, night was its entirely own entity.

At least, from what she'd been told.

She hadn't had a whole bunch of experience with this weather thing in Montana. She'd been here only three weeks and already she was really, really out of her depth.

And quite possibly in big, big trouble.

It didn't matter how hard Kate looked, pleaded, or shouted, her shadow remained stubbornly hidden.

No shadow, no answers from Grandma, certainly not about her heritage.

She reached up, the gesture so automatic, she barely noticed. How she traced the edge of her ear, felt the slight tip...such a slight difference, but enough to set her apart from everyone else, everyone she'd ever met.

At least until coming to Lighthome. Until meeting her grandmother, and James.

Kate brushed strands of her long, dark blond hair over her ears—also an automatic gesture—and shivered.

Not because of the chill, that wasn't exactly bothering her much, but being out here, in the forest...still not sure what was going to happen. But at least the dim lighting wasn't a problem; not a big one, anyway. She didn't *need* to watch where she was going as she moved through the dark forest, didn't need to take care with each and every step like any normal person would in the middle of the night, how they'd be stumbling about totally blind and helpless in the middle of this big, dark, foreboding forest.

A forest that also had a bit of a temperament issue.

Kate slipped past hidden logs, paused long enough to push a pine branch out of her way. No, she no longer needed a flashlight or even the moon, so that must mean she was getting the hang of this. Maybe not like Grandma or James, but...she was making progress. Right?

She could see just fine—or close enough.

Every day her low-light vision—at least, that was what James called it—improved. It wasn't perfect, and maybe if it had been, she'd have spotted her damn shadow already and this sneaking out wouldn't be necessary.

Well, not like she'd actually stop sneaking out. She needed time away from her grandmother to think. To breathe. To figure out what the hell was wrong with her life.

Or more to the point, what the hell she was.

Kate still had no idea how she exactly felt about *that*. Of being the descendant from some strange, mythical, elf-like beings her grand-mother was (mostly) keeping her lips zipped about. Which was why Kate needed to find her shadow—her spirit. It had been only a few days since her shadow (manifested via the not-very-happy-with-her-forest) had nearly devoured Kate.

She'd won a small respite from the forest—Alfeim Forest, to be exact—and she wasn't about to push it too far.

All of which meant she needed to scour every pine tree, pine cone, and rock looking for her stubborn, and very uncooperative, shadow.

Maybe, just maybe, if she found her shadow, the part of her that was still tied to the long-gone elves, almost like a spirit...an elven spirit, according to Grandma, a piece of them that, even over all these gener-ations, were still connected. And then maybe, once you found her elven spirit, she wouldn't feel quite so lost. Like maybe she would know what to do instead of just stumbling around, making all these mistakes.

She wasn't holding her breath—but she was determined to try.

Pine needles and scrunched-up leaves littered the small game trail. When she stepped there was no cracking or crunching sound. Just silence.

Creepy silence.

Maybe if a little luck dusted her way, she might even sneak back in the house without Grandma waking. Or, more specifically, if Grand-ma's ultrasonic special hearing didn't kick in and pull the old hag from whatever mythical dream she was having.

With her newly acknowledged gifts—not, she reminded herself, oddities that labeled her as "weird"—she spotted Grandma's house before passing the last tree cluster bordering Alfeim Forest.

Not like that was difficult, considering Grandma had turned on every porch light, gaslight, and lantern in Montana. The place lit up like a Christmas tree in mid-July. She might as well have put up a sign, "Kate—get your ass home now!"

Two months ago, when Kate's life had gone all topsy-turvy (with her nearly getting trapped and eaten by yet *another* forest), her mother had finally taken Kate to meet the grandmother she'd never seen or talked with before...and she then soon found herself living with said grandmother. Regardless, Kate had never been the type of girl who forced her mother to stay up late, watching the front door, fretting about what time it was or why Kate hadn't called. In truth, she needed actual friends to do that sort of thing and she'd only just turned seventeen, and being as weird as she was to everyone remotely close to her age, she hadn't exactly had a whole lot of opportunities for late nights, either.

But as far as Kate was concerned, she hadn't hit the "late" mark yet. Meaning it was before 2:00 AM.

Apparently, Grandma had other ideas.

Kate peeked through the shelter of pines and groaned. Maybe she'd be better off searching for her uncooperative and elusive shadow than going to bed.

Grandma lorded over the front porch, shotgun cocked, barrel out, waiting for Kate to return so she could shoot her ass.

Kate snorted. If she'd known what living with Grandma was like, she might have taken her mother up on the one-time, no-turning-around offer: leave with her and forget their silly little heritage.

Or stay and put up with Grandma.

At least her mother understood reason, whereas Grandma shot first and asked questions later.

"Quit sneakin' around there, Kate," Grandma growled. "And get yer ass back inside."

Of course she'd heard Kate—probably had know from a mile out that Kate was here.

"I will if you put the shotgun down."

She might have just met her grandmother only three weeks ago, but it hadn't taken long to realize just how trigger-happy her grandmother was.

Grandma frowned, her face easy for Kate to see from this distance. She could also make out her grandmother's slightly pointed ear as she tossed her gun—please God, let it not be loaded—onto the porch swing.

Adventures in living with an eighty-year-old crazy grandmother who also believed in elves, fairies, and whatever sort of mythical nonsense she could come up with.

Kate crept from the safety of her tree. Of course, if she hadn't met her grandmother, Kate wouldn't have met Yig, an ancient, talking ash tree who happened to like spending time with her.

Her shoulders slumped and she trudged the rest of the way. Definitely not the normal life she'd once dreamed of.

Grandma glared down at her, arms crossed, bright pink shawl wrapped around her as if she were naked underneath it or something. "Where the hell have you been? Is this how you treat your mother? Sneakin' off into the middle of the night?"

"No." She glared right back. "I didn't need to 'sneak' off when I lived with Mom."

Grandma's eyes did the furious-narrow thing and Kate could have sworn they flicked once to the shotgun.

"So you're startin' now? Is this something you learned from James? Trying to worry your old grandmother?"

"Yeah. Like you're old," Kate murmured.

Murmuring didn't matter much. She could have whispered the words, to the point where the breeze wouldn't have stirred, and her grandmother would still have heard.

"My tree rings are just fine," Grandma snapped. "I'm as old as any other old lady in the town."

Except those other old ladies couldn't swing a cane like Grandma. If Grandma used a cane, which she didn't.

Kate, however, took the diplomatic approach and said nothing. She merely crossed her arms and waited. If Grandma was as old as she claimed she was, then she'd be yawning any minute and it'd be off to bed.

Grandma didn't move. She leaned closer, as if knowing Kate's exact tactic, and Kate wondered if her mother had tried this back in the day. Anything was possible, especially considering her mom never talked about life here.

"What were you doin' out there?" Grandma nodded to the forest. "You know it's not safe."

She shrugged. "It's safe enough now. The forest isn't trying to eat me."

"You sure 'bout that?" Grandma spoke casually, almost taunting, but there was something underneath the words, something that made Kate step back.

James had told her she was safe. Her shadow—and the forest—had accepted her, had accepted her interest in her heritage. Had he lied?

"I was looking for my shadow."

"Your shadow. You went looking for your shadow. Tonight." Grandma's face paled. "You'd best get inside."

Kate paused, long enough to glance behind her. Nothing. No shadow, not even the moon's light. Nothing to explain why Grandma looked...so scared.

Best not to mention the previous nights. No point trying to unhinge her.

Grandma grabbed her gun and locked the door behind them. She even used the hundred-year-old, rusty deadbolt, then shooed Kate into the sitting room and then turned off all the lights... which, was weird.

Instead she headed straight for the fireplace.

"Grandma? What's going on?" Kate sat on the couch, though she had to scoot one of the old Labrador Retrievers, Jazz, over to make room. "What's wrong?"

"It's a good night for a fire, don't ya think?"

"Sure. I guess."

Since Kate had come to stay with her grandmother, she'd never seen the fireplace lit, even though there were always logs ready, and the small twigs she knew would help get the fire going. But as Grandma got to work, Kate's arms tingled.

It was a soft brush, the tiniest touch against her senses. She sat up straighter. A month ago, the feeling would have passed right over her. Not now. Not after everything she'd learned so far.

"Grandma?"

Grandma hunched over the fireplace, hands moving in the air. Kate didn't see a match or a lighter, not even a little gas knob in the brick to explain the sudden—and she did mean sudden—blaze of flame.

Kate jumped back and smacked into the sleeping Jazz. The fire roared up the chimney, flames stretching higher than she'd thought possible.

"Fires are good for these nights."

Grandma rose, her knees cracking. Besides her white hair and wrinkled face, there was no other signs of her age. Grandma blazed like the fire.

Kate blinked back tears and knew something was going on here. Too bad she had no idea what it was.

"Fires are good, because they help us see beyond the veil."

"The veil?"

"A boundary, if you will, separating our world and theirs…"

Grandma waved her hands towards the flame.

"What world?"

Grandma sighed and suddenly her youth, the light shining from her, dimmed. The older woman was back, though her shoulders drooped a bit more than they had when she'd waited on the porch, shotgun tucked neatly in her armpit.

"In truth, if the stories are true, the veil separates all worlds. Don't matter which you believe in, Norse or Irish mythology or the half-dozen others that got trampled on and beaten out through the long years. The veil is still one and the same. It keeps our world separated from the others. Spirit worlds, magic worlds and, important to our story: the world our elven ancestors came from. The world your mother ran away from."

Hope flared through Kate. "Tell me."

"That, dear, is part of the problem. I don't know how."

Grandma picked up her shotgun from where she'd laid it, cracked open the barrel and took out the two shells.

Holy shit. It *had* been loaded.

"Well, how about you starting at the beginning?"

After all, didn't all stories start there?

Grandma snorted. "Not even your tree friend could remember the beginning and he's old, much older than our ancestors. Yggdrasil." She snorted. "Never thought *he'd* show up on this side of the veil, but hey, just tells you we know a whole lot about nothin'."

"He prefers the name Yig."

Grandma snorted again, as if the thought were both funny and unbelievable. Not that Kate fully understood the big deal about her friend, this old, talking tree with his spotty memory.

"Anyway," Grandma said, "the forest itself might be young, you know, in terms of earth age and whatnot, but Alfeim—what it truly *is*—is not young."

Kate swallowed a snort of her own. Grandma *was* trying to be helpful here.

Right?

"You're gonna have to be more specific than that."

"Our ancestors weren't the only ones who crossed the veil. Alfeim, at least parts of it, well, it crossed with them. Maybe your pal Yig was one of them, or maybe it was already here. But definitely Alfeim."

"The forest? You're saying it's from another world."

And no, there was no hiding the sarcasm in her voice; it *was* just a tad bit unbelievable.

"And hence our little problem," Grandma said. "You think I, and all the rest of us, are crazy."

Grandma dropped the two shotgun shells in the pocket of her nightgown, then propped the gun against the wall. Still within easy reach, Kate noticed.

"Crazy or not, that's your call to make, but I warn you, your shadow, Katherine Silver, you must be careful of it. I don't know how else to explain to you. Yes, the shadow—and Alfeim Forest—have accepted you, but you haven't accepted them yet. Otherwise, well, it wouldn't be a shadow anymore."

She wanted to jump up and shake her grandmother until she told her everything. *Everything.*

"What about you? How did your parents tell you?"

Kate's words, anxious and fast, leapt from her mouth. She wanted to know, wanted to understand her family, the family her mother had refused to even acknowledge, let alone discuss.

"It's not so simple," Grandma said. "The world was different back then. My parents believed and, therefore, I believed. There was no debate, no disagreements."

Grandma waved her hand in the place where a TV would have stood, at least if this were a normal American household. Actually, there'd be at least three TVs.

"It was a different world back then, not like now. If my daddy was angry, he'd grab the nearest belt and I'd cry for all I was worth. If I were smart, I'd learn."

"Your dad hit you?"

"See?" Grandma pointed at Kate. "Probably never been spanked in yer life. No wonder you've got the issues you have now."

"I hardly see how my mother not spanking me has anything to do with my shadow."

"It has everything to do with it." Grandma sank into her rocking chair, the wood smooth from constant use. "I can't just prop my feet up, pour us some beer, and tell you the stories—the stories my parents shared with me. Stories my parents believed."

In truth, Kate could probably go for a beer right now. She might be underage, but these were desperate circumstances here. But she waited, pretending patience.

"Why not? Why can't you just tell me?"

"It don't work that way. Not if you're to believe. Not if you're to survive."

Grandma leaned closer, eyes piercing Kate. For a moment, Grandma's light had returned. It filled her eyes, her body, then faded.

Grandma had said it was a different world. Did she mean culture? Probably.

Kate glanced around the room, the stuffed deer trophies, the stack of fur blankets against the worst of winter's chill. It was a home that'd been in their family since forever—according to Grandma. It was the kind of home, Kate thought, where you could believe in fairy tales and legends.

The kind of world where elves were real and trees talked.

Kate didn't come from this world and somehow, that meant she couldn't see her shadow. "Did you have a shadow?"

Grandma shook her head. "My shadow and I were always one and the same. I accepted my spirit, my ancestors. Back then, we all did. It wasn't until later, until your mother's time, when our world shifted. We didn't see it at first, didn't recognize it for it was."

"And that's when the shadows appeared?"

"It's when we started losin' some kids, them disappearing into the forest." Grandma squeezed her eyes closed and it was several minutes before she opened them again.

Kate wanted to ask why, wanted to ask what memory caused her such pain.

"I lost your mother, even though she returned from the forest, even though the forest let her leave. I don't want to lose you."

Kate slid off the couch and touched her grandmother's knee. "If you tell me, then maybe —"

"I told your mother and look where it got me? 'Course, how was I supposed to know she'd hooked up with some magi. Damn people weren't even supposed to exist anymore."

Grandma clicked her mouth closed as if she'd said something she shouldn't have.

"Magi?"

"Oh, hell," Grandma cursed. "That, there, that was old age creepin' in and you took advantage."

Oh, no. She wasn't getting away that easily. "Who are the magi? Who did my mother meet?"

Grandma stood, shooing Kate away. "They're no good, that's who they are, and none are worse than the one your mother hooked up with. Our kind and theirs don't mix well. We'll get to those bastards in good time, but right now we need you to accept your shadow. It's best for you and this is the only way I can teach what you need."

Grandma grabbed Kate's arm and hauled her towards the fire. "Only one way to see if you've opened yerself enough."

That was how Kate found herself kneeling on the hard stone floor, staring at a very hot, and very close, fire. "How is this supposed to help me?"

Honestly, she couldn't help the sarcasm leaking from her. Different cultures, remember?

Grandma frowned, lips pinched in a tight line. Probably thinking whether or not she should spank Kate.

She didn't, which Kate thought was a bonus.

"The answer is here, in the fire." Grandma waved towards it, her spindly fingers dancing in time with the flames.

That wasn't very helpful. "Can you give me some more clues? Maybe a hint of what I should be looking for?"

"Yourself."

AS FAR AS ADVICE WENT, looking for "herself" was pretty lame. And pretty useless.

Kate groaned, shifting her weight from one knee to the other. At this point, even her cheater pillow felt like a rock. And the fire was still just a fire; nothing at all special that she could see.

In truth, this was Kate's second fire, as she'd given up some time last night. She'd stared until her knees, her hands, and her brain had gone numb and mushy. But she tried. She really did. Even when Grandma sighed and told her it was useless and to go to bed, Kate had stayed.

She'd kept trying and kept failing, which was no different than how this second attempt was going.

Part of her had hoped that being tired would somehow trigger her sleeping magical abilities or something. Or at least make it so her conscious brain would take a hike.

When that failed, except for the falling-asleep part, Kate had stormed out the next day looking for advice, and since Grandma was her usual old and stubborn self (especially when Kate brought up the magi again), Kate went to the one person who could help.

Kate asked Yig.

If she was feeling fair and gracious—which she wasn't—Kate would admit Yig had given her some good advice. Okay, maybe it wasn't great advice, but he'd at least given her some direction.

"Your grandmother was correct. Fire is the easiest path to see between worlds."

Okay, that particular part wasn't very helpful.

Kate grabbed a log and shoved it on top of the shrinking fire. Immediately sparks crackled pink and blue colors. She had no idea why, other than the possibility that Grandma had sprinkled in some chemical to make it look like magic.

But that wasn't like Grandma's style. Sure, Grandma was evasive, but she wasn't deceptive—not like Kate's mother was.

"Focus." Yig's voice tickled Kate's memory as if he were there beside her, knowing she was indeed not focusing. *"You will never succeed, will never become one with your shadow, if you do not open your mind."*

Kate tossed a smaller twig into the fire. This one didn't spark like the log. She got what Yig was telling her. If Kate couldn't accept the possibility of magic, accept that she might possibly be a descendant from some ancient elf, then she might as well pack her bags and go home.

She wanted to change. She just didn't know how.

"Yes, you do." Kate growled.

Both Grandma and Yig had told her how. Time to buck up and give it a serious try.

Of course, this probably included her sarcastic thoughts about deep breaths and her visions of a white padded room.

At least she was alone, other than the two dogs snoring away in the fire's radiating warmth. It was as if that thought, her being completely alone, meant she could relax.

And for once, Kate didn't question it, and let her shoulders droop forward, let her breathing deepen. After a few minutes of turning off her mind, of thinking about nothing but breathing, she was surprised she actually felt good. Maybe Yig was onto something.

As Yig had instructed, Kate thought about the veil separating these two worlds. One world, her own, she understood, but this other one? She hadn't a clue. But that was part of the journey, she thought, this discovery. If she was starting on any journey, she'd have to start at the beginning.

Kate imagined herself opening the door. She took a deep breath and walked through, her feet stirring the small pile of leaves. The scent of pine and open air surrounded her, but she couldn't see the path, couldn't see where she was going.

Which left Kate with only two options. She could either go back or she could do the stupid thing and walk into the forest, by herself, in the pitch dark.

Clearly sunlight didn't apply to vision journeys or quests or whatever the heck this was. Kate hoped she was making the right (or at least not stupid) decision and strode into the creepy forest.

If she'd thought it was dark before, she was woefully mistaken. The light vanished and now she really didn't want to go forward.

This was a dream, nothing more. So why the hell was she suddenly so scared?

Amazingly, she didn't trip over anything. Her body, her senses, seemed to know when exactly to shift to the side, when to pick up her foot, and when to suddenly duck.

She scrambled over a boulder, feeling for grooves to stick her feet in, to pull herself over. And once she got to the top, after chipping her nails and scraping her hands, she had another problem. Somehow, she had to get down.

A rustle of feathers echoed in the darkness, as if a great bird had landed somewhere nearby in the trees. That sudden sway of pine needles as talons reached out and grabbed a branch, followed by a flap or two as the bird settled itself.

But no matter how hard Kate squinted, all she saw was the same darkness.

"I've come this far." And she jumped.

The soft earth cushioned her feet as she stumbled, and when she looked up, expecting to see darkness, found herself in a familiar grove.

Yig's grove.

Two rows of old pines lined the path, their branches bending and creaking as they shifted—no *gestured*—to the center. Giant wings flapped once, then twice.

She spun, squinting to see where the bird was, but saw nothing but trees and branches. And got the sudden sense that this bird was following her.

The closer Kate got, the more she realized something wasn't right. Not wrong exactly, but not right, either.

Yes, it was Yig with his giant, high, arching crown and his gnarled, twisted, and still beautiful trunk. The light shifted from muted gray to shimmering colors.

Yig's eyes, what Kate thought of as eyes, cracked open at her approach. The moss clumps lifted, revealing two large knobs. He looked...tired. Moreso than she remembered.

"Yig? Are you okay?"

His branches swayed more, as if stretching. *"Ah, Little Eagle. You've found your way to me."*

"Well, yeah. I mean, I knew the path." 'Course, she'd never tried walking in the pitch black before.

"You had known one way, but you did not know both ways."

"Both ways?" She held her breath. Realization of what she'd done— or might have done—filtered through her.

She wanted to scan the trees, the darker shadows, and search for her own shadow. She didn't.

Somehow, it didn't feel right. That if she searched, it wouldn't be right.

"There are always two paths, sometimes more, but always two." The twisted bark of his lip lowered. A smile. *"But yes, you found the way. You have entered the veil. And you now see me as I am. Not the truth, but closer to it."*

Kate slipped closer and sat on her favorite root. There were three like it, all giant and penetrating deep into the earth. This one, however, had the perfect indention for her butt.

"You look the same. I mean, you look more tired, but even that moss sticking out of your nose. Is the same."

Kate pointed, realized what she'd just said, and apologized. "I mean, I didn't..."

Yig chuckled. Yes, this ancient ash tree chuckled at her. Kate smiled back. Okay, it was a little funny, and he probably hadn't had someone point out his "nose" hairs in quite a few millennia.

If the elves even discussed this sort of thing, but she doubted it.

Yig's chuckle faded, and he lowered a branch and gently touched her arm. She didn't back away or flinch. For some reason, it comforted Kate.

"You still see me this way because you have not fully learned to let go," Yig

said. *"You've found your way, but this is only the start. To see me as I truly am, to see yourself and your grandmother as Truth, requires much more."*

"Well, shit. Coming this far was hard enough." And she wasn't sure how much more fire-staring her knees could handle.

"What is you wish for, Little Eagle? Why did you search the fire?"

"I wanted to find my shadow."

"But why?"

She didn't think "Grandma told me to" was the answer Yig was looking for.

This was the question Grandma hadn't asked Kate. Grandma hadn't asked why. Maybe she didn't want to know. Maybe she was afraid of the answer.

"Little Eagle?"

Kate dug her fingers into the dirt and squeezed. The earth was warm and soft, comforting. Real. She needed real right now; only real could give her that tiny bit of strength.

Enough strength to speak the truth.

"My shadow knows. It knows the truth about my heritage, about the forest...about me."

Kate glanced up at Yig, who'd bent closer, his crown looking like it'd topple onto her any minute. "I knew if I found my shadow, then I might learn the truth."

Yig's bushy, mossy eyebrows lifted. *"I see. And yes, your shadow does indeed know these truths."*

Kate released the dirt, ignoring the clumps under her fingernails. "It doesn't matter, though. I haven't seen my shadow and I'm back where I started."

"You are so sure?"

Her head snapped up. "What do you mean?"

"How do you think you found me if you did not have help? If you did not have a guide?"

Kate stumbled to her feet, her body suddenly not working the way it was supposed to. Was it true?

She searched the shadows, scanning the tree trunks, and didn't see anything....

A gentle flap of wings. A stationary flap, not the flying kind. Movement meant to draw her attention.

Afraid, anxious, and almost wanting to pee in her pants, Kate turned towards the sound. Whatever happened, whatever she saw, she'd be okay.

Kate's mouth went dry.

Yig called her "Little Eagle," but she'd had no idea he was telling her the truth. Telling her who she was.

What her spirit was.

There, perched on Yig's branches, was a bald eagle. Majestic white head, eyes that pierced through Kate. The eagle raised his wings outward and flapped once, twice.

Saying hello.

Grandma hadn't told Kate proper protocol upon meeting her spirit guide, so she bowed. "I'm really glad to finally meet you."

When she straightened, the eagle's eyes met hers. Something inside her shifted, clicked into place. Her vision cleared and the shadowy grove grew brighter and vibrant with colors and life.

The eagle raised his head and greeted her. His scream echoed through the forest, sharp and powerful, and completely beautiful.

Warmth rose in front of her face and sweat trickled down her neck and into her shirt. A fire.

She watched as Yig closed his eyes, watched as her eagle launched from his branch and flew off. She tried to follow, tried to see where he was going, but the forest faded.

No darkness this time, only the bright red of flames.

Kate opened her eyes and found herself back in Grandma's living room, the fire blazing hot.

"Ah, you're back."

Kate turned and saw Grandma in her rocking chair, knitting needles clicking as she wove together some hideous fuchsia yarn.

"Grandma?"

And out of all the questions Kate could ask, she picked the one her overloaded mind could handle:

"I didn't know you could knit."

"There are quite a few things this old lady can do, and quite a few not even your mother knows about."

Grandma cracked a smile, then chuckled, just as Yig had done. But unlike Yig, there was bit of a nervous tone to it and her face...it was a bit pale, even in the warm, orange-yellow light of the fire.

"Are you okay?"

Grandma put down her needles but stayed in her chair, rocking and back and forth, thinking, clearly, but her eyes never left Kate's. And the paleness in her face, well, that didn't change much either.

"Your journey went well."

"Yeah." Kate shifted and groaned. Her poor, abused knees.

"Happens, even to the young ones." And as if that was all the explanation Kate needed, Grandma went back to knitting. "Either way, it looks like you had a long walk. There's some dinner in the fridge. You can heat it up on the stove."

"Thanks." Kate stretched, reaching her arms over her head. "How long was I sitting there?"

"Awhile."

"You're not even going to ask what happened? Weren't you worried about me?"

Grandma closed her eyes. A shiver passed over her.

Finally she opened them and shook her head. "No, no, I'm not. Your vision quest is yours and it's none of my—or anyone else's—business. As to your second question..."

Grandma pointed at the front door with her needles. "I knew you were fine."

"Why?"

"Well, there's a rather good-sized bald eagle perched on our front tree."

Kate ran towards the door, ignoring her aching knees, and thrust open the screen door.

A bald eagle, just like she'd seen in Yig's grove, preened its feathers on the tallest branch. An eagle who'd clearly waited for Kate.

The eagle lowered its wing and turned towards her. Kate smiled, even as she heard the familiar, comforting scream.

She waved and noticed the dirt under her nails. It hadn't been a dream.

"What happened to you there," Grandma whispered, "it wasn't

what I expected. Don't think anyone in a hundred years and more would have expected. You found your shadow all right, and I think… more besides."

"Because of Yig?"

"Because of the veil, Kate, and the path you took to reach him."

Grandma placed a hand on her shoulder, the same place Yig had touched her. Her touch was warm, though, comforting. A touch that Kate knew, whatever happened, would always be there for her.

Unlike her mother.

"It's a start," Grandma said. "You're not there yet, but it's a start."

Grandma's worry, her fear, it was still clear as day in her eyes, but there was also something else…pride… something Kate wasn't used to seeing. Not in herself, certainly not from her mother.

She nodded, though, and felt that same pride swell within her chest. She'd done it. She'd found her shadow…and now, her elven spirit. Or, at least, a piece of it. There was still more to learn, still more to unlock and understand, but it all just felt right, like a lock slowly clicking open in her chest.

"And hopefully," Kate said, "one step closer to finding answers. Unless, of course, you want to make this easy and just tell me."

"Life ain't easy." Grandma patted her shoulder and her familiar, cranky grandmother was back. "Not even us elven-folk descendants. But you keep going and you'll find yourself some answers, maybe even a few you wouldn't want to find."

"It'd be the truth, though."

That was what mattered; that was all she ever wanted. The truth of who she was.

Just as in the grove beside the aging house, her eagle raised his wings—easily the same length as her arms—and disappeared into the night. His farewell cry echoed behind him, but she knew it wasn't farewell.

She smiled. One step closer to the truth, even if it meant traversing through fire vision quests and learning to speak eagle.

Where she went from here, Kate hadn't a clue, but she imagined her grandma had a few unhelpful and cryptic hints waiting for her.

At least Kate had found her spirit guide. She'd found herself.

SNEAK PEAK: HIDDEN IN TIME

An Elven Heritage Novel

CHAPTER ONE

Kate took another slow step, her hiking boots pressing into the soft, spongy grass. She shivered as a cooling breeze drifted up and around the tall trunks of pine trees and larches and a whole bunch of others whose names she didn't know (and frankly, didn't care a whole lot about either).

She wanted to stay.

To sit on that boulder right there, overlooking that slow-moving creek, with water that had a hint of aqua to it. Fresh and cold from all the glaciers melting way off and up there in the distance, nestled up in those dark mountain peaks. She'd sprawl, arms and legs stretched out on that rock, with its mix of pink and black and ruddy-brown specks. Close her eyes. Feel the last bit of warmth from both the rock and the sun until, finally, she fell into a comfortable, peaceful rest.

After all, it *had* been a long, long three days of hiking. Camping. Trudging up some mountain in the middle of nowhere Montana, in the middle of July, sweat pouring out of just about every pore, all to help her understand her heritage.

Oh, and totally skipping on the showering bit. Or the simple washing of her hair.

Ugh.

Her hair *used* to be this darker blond color, nice sunlight gold streaks, about the only attractive feature. Now though... well, her hair looked more like the forest floor, what with all the twigs and leaves and tangles she'd acquired since she'd started this oh-so-lovely camping expedition into the wilderness of Alfeim.

And yet, even with her missing all those oh, so important amenities, she wanted to stay.

Stay right here, in this small glade with its trickling creek and canopy of pine needles, the way the trees and their branches bowed to her, their bark and joints creaking as if they'd been asleep for an age, but finally, because of her, were waking up.

The glade didn't want her to go either.

She felt it.

Felt the trees, who were sad to see her leave. Even the grass, somehow still holding onto moisture from the morning dew all those hours ago, and how the heck there was any moisture at all was certainly some kind of magic (she had the sweat-soaked T-shirt to prove just how damn hot and dry it got during the day). That grass though, magic or not, with all its small individual blades, gave her a final, wet tickling along her ankles, right where her wool socks couldn't quite reach.

The last of the setting sun cast a dusting of gold specks in the air as if it, too, were waving goodbye.

Above her, circling high up overhead in the hot thermals and wind currents, was Eagle. His great brown wings stretched out as he rode the hot thermals and wind currents of that endless sky, with all those purples and pinks blending until finally fading into darkness.

Simply beautiful. All of it.

Kate breathed in, feeling the peace of this place, the peace she was finally feeling within herself. About her unique heritage. About the warm, new candlelight glowing within her.

And there, right in the middle of that endless sky, stretching out across the whole it seemed, was Eagle. His brilliant white head a beacon, ready to lead her home.

Eagle gave a sad, shrill cry.

He knew her well, her spirit guide. Always there for her, always watching out for her. And now, telling her it was time to leave.

Kate's stomach twisted.

Just a little, but enough. Enough to know that, by taking this one last step, she'd be leaving a part of herself behind.

Which, in a way, she was.

This wasn't her glade, exactly. It was Kátheryn's.

Kátheryn Silverstar, the warm candlelight within her.

The soft pink and gold flame. Still small, just like an actual candle flame, but growing stronger. And Kate had a feeling that the real Kátheryn probably felt more like a high school bonfire.

But now, more than ever, Kate understood why she'd always felt so different. So weird and strange.

She *was* different. Yes, she was an elf-descendant, just like her mom, just like her grandma, and also, a bit more. Like, an actual elven soul living right beside hers.

That's right. Not just one, but two souls.

Cause her life couldn't get anymore complicated with it just being *her* in there.

Her, the recently-turned seventeen-year-old who'd been seen as odd and weird everywhere she went, every house she'd lived in, every school she'd been forced into. The reaction, the treatment, by her classmates, teachers too, always the same. Her slightly pointed ears and crazy-good hearing really didn't help. Then there was her mom, Queen of Denial and Running, who'd pretty much dumped her out in the wilds of Montana with a crazy Grandma who, while she was crazy, had a certain fondness for shotguns and a history that you'd never, ever find in history books.

Like tales straight out of myths. Probably legends, if you believed in that sort of thing.

Like... well, like Kátheryn.

Kátheryn Silverstar who was the other part of Kate, the part that had *really* made her seem 'other' to just about every person she met. Except for Grandma. And James.

Kátheryn, the long-dead elf soul whose glade Kate now stood in.

This place had once been her home... a really, really long time ago, but it was pretty apparent that the glade, and the trees, probably even the ants crawling up that branch not two inches from her head, remembered her.

Kátheryn, that was.

Not Kate.

And she had to leave. Had to leave this beautiful, peaceful place. A place where she could well and truly hide, where all the bad things out there couldn't get her, from her evil-ass dad to the sore heart she just knew she'd feel the second she caught a glimpse of James again.

Because... she had to get back to camp. To warn Grandma about James's bitch of a mom and the war she wanted to start between the magi and the elf-descendants. A warning Kate had gotten because of Kátheryn and her magic, and the memory from Alfeim Forest itself.

There was still so much Kate didn't know about her heritage, about who she was, or heck, even what she could do. And Kátheryn, she'd shown Kate just a little bit more. How to connect with Alfeim Forest, its consciousness, to feel the actual shifting of the earth as it breathed, the small worms and bugs digging down there amidst the roots. And by doing so, she'd been able to see the forest Memory. A memory as if she'd been standing right there, watching the whole thing unfold.

A memory and a warning, one that she needed to share. She had to tell James, even if he'd end up hating her for it.

Eagle called to her again. Urging her and a little... uneasy it felt like. Like he needed her to move. To hurry.

Yes, it was time to go.

"I'm sorry," Kate whispered.

Though, she didn't know if she spoke to the glade or that slight tightening in her chest. An ache that she felt like it was splitting her in two.

Not that she could blame Kátheryn. After all, just waking up from a really long sleep and learning the person whose eyes you stared out was actually a pretty pathetic version of an elf-descendant, who was bad at just about *everything* elvish.

Like magic.

Especially magic.

Which was just another truth she couldn't run from. Not any

longer. Couldn't be her mom, who just kept running and driving and hiding. Oh, and lots of denying.

Not Kate. Never, Kate.

At least, not anymore.

Eagle flew on ahead, straight into that sunset. Kate followed him, followed the golden strand that always connected them. She took one last look at the glade, this place that felt like home and called to just about every inch of her being. The sun finished its descent, giving her one last, golden wink.

She took that final step—

Her boots sank straight down into a giant mound of freezing, brilliant white snow. And her connection to Eagle, her beautiful spirit guide, with his constant warmth and love, who believed in her when no one would, snapped.

To continue reading, go to ChrissyWissler.com or your favorite bookseller.

AN IMPATIENT FOREST. ONE STUBBORN GIRL.

Let the battle begin.

An expert at ignoring problems, Kate Silver focuses on her giant-sized bowl of ice cream. Double-scoop of huckleberry, cookies n' cream, sprinkles, river of hot fudge.

No problems at all.

Except for her backpack zinging with magic. And the impatient, unhappy tree tapping at her window.

Ignore an angry forest? Not a good idea.

Hidden in Darkness, a story about a reluctant girl coming to terms with herself and the magic living inside her—whether or not she wants it. The "In-Between" Elven Heritage Story, set some time after the events in *Hidden in Time*.

By joining my list you'll receive wonderful benefits such as being notified of upcoming book releases as well as the never-before-published short story and special gift for fans of the series: *Hidden in Darkness*.

To enjoy your free copy of *Hidden in Darkness* and keep up with the latest news and releases, go to https://dl.bookfunnel.com/yk3ksnyz29 and chrissywissler.com.

ABOUT THE AUTHOR

Chrissy Wissler's writing has garnered praise both from readers and professional writers. Readers love her characters and the emotional grip she engenders.

About her novel *Home Run*, *New York Times* bestselling author Kristine Kathryn Rusch said: "Wonderful book, chockfull of unexpected surprises. If you like sports novels, you'll like this—even if you don't like romance. If you like romance, you'll like this—even if you don't like sports novels."

Chrissy's short fiction has appeared in the anthologies: *Fiction River: Risk-Takers, Fiction River Presents: Legacies, Fiction River Presents: Readers' Choice, Deep Magic,* and *When Dreams Come True*. She writes fantasy and science fiction, as well as a softball, contemporary series for both romance and young adult.

Before turning to fiction, Chrissy also wrote nonfiction for publications such as *Montana Outdoors, Women in the Outdoors,* and *Jakes Magazine*. In 2009, *Inside Kung Fu* magazine awarded her with their 'Writer of the Year' award.

Follow her online at ChrissyWissler.com, as well as her blog on being a parent-writer, at ParentsandProse.

To enjoy another story by Chrissy Wissler and to keep up with the latest news, releases and more, go to: chrissywissler.com/free-book/

For more information:
www.chrissywissler.com
chrissy@chrissywissler.com

ALSO BY CHRISSY WISSLER

Elven Heritage Series

Hidden in Mist

Hidden in Truth

Hidden in Shadow

Hidden in Fire

Hidden in Flight

Hidden in Spirit

Hidden in Desire

Hidden in Memory

Hidden in Time: Novel

Hidden in Lore: Collection #1

Hidden in Myth: Collection #2

Hidden in Legend: Collection #3

Little League Series

Swing Away: A Little League Novel

Prom Dates & Softball Bats

Throw Like a Girl, Catch a Date

Fly Away

No Crying in Softball

More to Life than Softball

A Pitcher's Unexpected Date

A Catcher's Christmas Wish

Stolen Bases, Stolen Kisses

Softball Baby